D1561567

Easton at
CHRISTMASTIDE
Book Five in *The Easton* Series

ENDORSEMENTS

In the midst of personal challenges, an unexpected gift from the past connects Erin with her grandfather, Peter Kichline, hero of the Revolutionary War. Surprises await the reader in this page-turner of a book by beloved award-winning author Rebecca Price Janney. *Easton at Christmastide* is perfect for everyone on your holiday list!
—Linda Texter Hall, Poet and Essayist

Rebecca Price Janney has a unique way of combining heart-warming stories with historical accuracy. *Easton at Christmastide* proves no different. The story will undoubtedly convict you, inspire you, and encourage you to look at our history through a different lens.
—Arch Hunter, Director of Graduate Programs, Freedoms Foundation

The author has a wonderful ability to bring her characters to life, both historical and modern. A must for Christmas giving or reading.
—Bobbi McMullen, Pennsylvania DAR Honorary State Regent

Rebecca is a beautiful storyteller whose ability to help the reader transcend time and space to understand Peter and Erin's linked experiences, victories, and struggles is

again evident in her fifth book in the Easton Series. Rebecca encourages us to think differently about our American Story. *Easton at Christmastide* is a timely release and a must-read!
—**Brooke Mitman**, Founder, Restoration Media

I so enjoyed this Christmas addition to the Easton Series! In her signature way, Janney seamlessly weaves stories of past and present into a compelling, cohesive story, rich with historical detail and enhanced with late 18th century journal entries from Peter Kichline. *Easton at Christmastide* will be an excellent addition to your holiday reading! What a nice ending, and a great book.
—**Marlo Schalesky**, Author of Women of the Bible Speak Out

Family dynamics, family ancestry, history and Christmas—an outstanding combination that equals a good read of historic fiction. The story of Erin, her present and the past, touch the heart and give hope. Peter Kichline, her ancestor, reaches through time with a unique artifact to shine light on Erin and her family. Open this book and become involved with the dynamics of the Easton community past and present; you will enjoy being a witness as their stories entwine through the pages. Don't miss this latest addition to the Easton saga!
—**Cyndy Sweeney**, NSDAR Librarian General, 2019-2022

The diary of an important ancestor arrives unexpectedly—a soldier in the American Revolution—sending a modern writer on a quest to unravel a family mystery. This delightful tale of intrigue is told by Rebecca Price Janney, weaving today's world with the momentous events that gave birth to America. It's yet another great story in the award-winning Easton Series!
—**Dr. Craig von Buseck**, award-winning author and host of the Stories & Myths program.

Easton at Christmastide is a delightful addition to the Easton Series. Rebecca Price Janney takes the reader from the present to the colonial period of our history then back again as she personalizes the characters in the book, puts flesh on their bones, and provides the readers a new appreciation for the sacrifices of our ancestors. If you enjoy historical novels, genealogy, faith, and family, brew a cup of tea and savor this marvelous book.

—Lynn Forney Young

Easton at
CHRISTMASTIDE
Book Five in *The Easton* Series

Rebecca Price Janney

PUBLISHING THE POSITIVE
Plymouth, Massachusetts

COPYRIGHT NOTICE

Cover and Interior Design: Derinda Babcock
Photo of Peter Kichline Courtesy of Paul Strikwerda
Editor: Deb Haggerty
Author Represented By: WordWise Media Services

PUBLISHED BY: Elk Lake Publishing, Inc., 35 Dogwood Drive, Plymouth, MA 02360, 2021

Library Cataloging Data

Names: Janney, Rebecca Price (Rebecca Price Janney)
Easton at Christmastide—Book Five in the Easton Series / Rebecca Price Janney
284 p. 23cm × 15cm (9in × 6 in.)

ISBN-13: 978-1-64949411-5 (paperback) | 978-1-64949-412-2 (trade paperback) | 978-1-64949-413-9 (e-book)

Key Words: Pennsylvania, Patriots, Romance, Holiday Celebrations, American Revolution, Time Slip Novel, 1700s

Library of Congress Control Number: 2021948481 Fiction

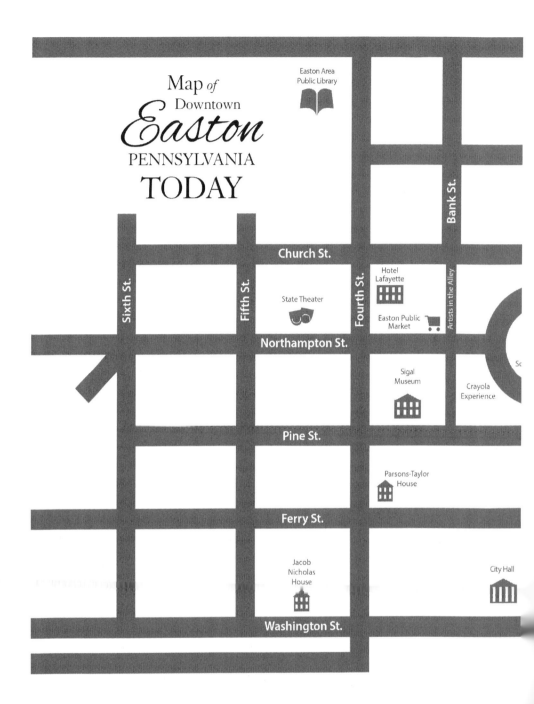

Map *of*
Downtown
Easton
PENNSYLVANIA
TODAY

Easton Area
Public Library

Bank St.

Church St.

Sixth St.

Fifth St.

Fourth St.

State Theater

Hotel
Lafayette

Artists in the Alley

Easton Public
Market

Northampton St.

Sigal
Museum

Crayola
Experience

Pine St.

Parsons-Taylor
House

Ferry St.

Jacob
Nicholas
House

City Hall

Washington St.

Lehigh River

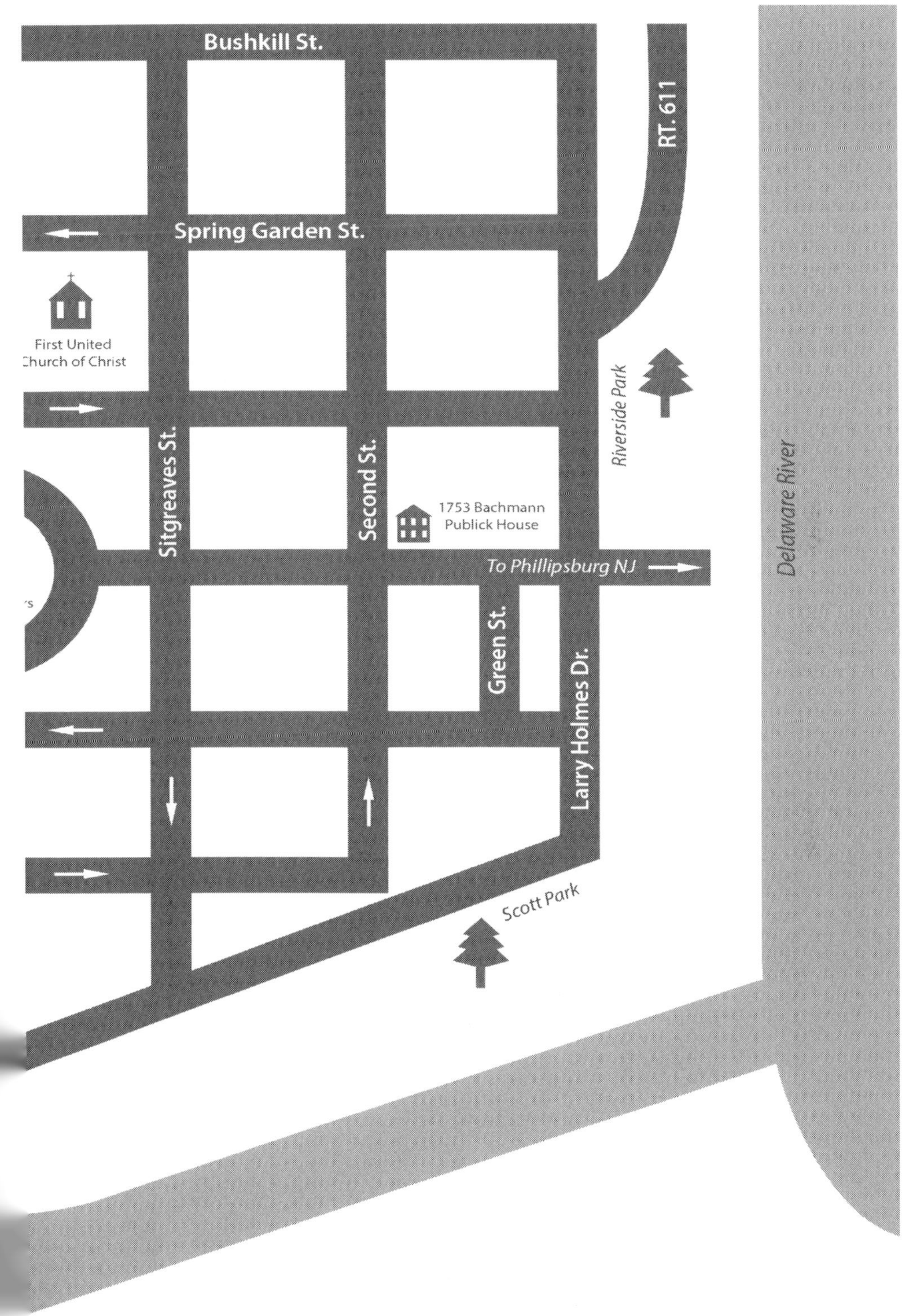
Bushkill St.
RT. 611
Spring Garden St.
First United
Church of Christ
Riverside Park
Sitgreaves St.
Second St.
1753 Bachmann
Publick House
To Phillipsburg NJ
Delaware River
Green St.
Larry Holmes Dr.
Scott Park

Map

of

Easton

PENNSYLVANIA

1776

Reformed
Burial Ground

Hamilton St.

Jacob Opp's
Tavern

Northampton St.

Peter
Kichline

Lewis
Gordon

Julianna St.

The Old
Parsons

Ferry

Lutl
Bu
Gro

Lehigh River

Bushkill St.

Spring Garden St.

Pomfret St.

The Reformed-Lutheran Church

Henry Fullert

Dr Ledlie

Stable

Fermor St.

Shannon's Tavern

The Courthouse

Meyer Hart's Store

Ferry House & Tavern

The Ferry

Delaware River

DEDICATION:

This story is for my beloved readers,
who are a precious gift to me.

ACKNOWLEDGMENTS

Like the gifts of Christmas whose sweetness lingers long after we open the last of our presents, blessings have abounded from many sources throughout the months of writing this latest story in the *Easton Series*.

Many thanks to my Elk Lake Publishing team, editor-par-excellence Deb Haggerty, book designer Derinda Babcock, audiobook ace Travis "Will" Inman, and Michael Hollingsworth, who brings these stories to life. (I just love your German accent!)

My agent and brother in Christ Dave Fessenden challenges me to excellence and encourages my efforts, and his wife Jacque cheers me on while offering her own expert feedback. Thank you also to Steve Hutson of WordWise Media Services.

I am grateful for the abiding love and affection of my dream team, Scott and David Janney, and my faithful sidekick Perry.

I wouldn't be able to keep this series going without my loyal readers, and I love each of you dearly.

Finally, where would I be without the Christ Child? I don't want to know.

Rebecca Price Janney
Christmas, 2021

The people walking in darkness
have seen a great light;
on those living in the land of deep darkness
a light has dawned.
Isaiah 9:2 (NIV)

EPIC FAILURE—AMAZING GRACE

CHAPTER ONE

Erin had every reason to despise Connie Pierce, including this latest travesty. As she stood there with a Dollar Store bag dragging from her right hand, hair still damp from the shower, Erin gaped at a dining room table teaming with wrapping paper, gift bags, ribbon, bows, tape, and scissors, arranged in assembly-line fashion. Completed presents perched on a side table, worthy of a Fifth Avenue display and presided over by their salon-perfect mistress.

Connie rushed over to Erin and administered a perfunctory hug, which Erin did not lean into. "Please excuse the mess." She swept her hand over the table, then smoothed an imaginary stray lock of hair over her right eye.

"I would if I could see one."

Their eyes met, and Erin blushed, wishing she could take back her harsh tone.

A giggle seemed to catch in Connie's throat and came out as a croak. "I'm just finishing the last of my Christmas presents."

This is just too much. Not only has she finished buying presents, she's wrapping them too. It's November first, for Pete's sake.

"I'm a little behind this year." Connie's hands trembled as she picked up a medium-sized box and affixed the last of the tape along the sides. "Normally I buy gifts throughout the year, whenever I see something that reminds me of someone, and that way I avoid the last-minute rush in the stores. I try to be finished by mid-October, but this year it's taken until the day after Halloween. I guess I've been too busy."

Erin gaped, her mouth an open mailbox with nothing inside.

"Those must be the C.A.R.'s contribution for the gift bags." Connie inclined her head toward her visitor's parcel.

She yearned to end this visit as quickly as possible, the once-soothing vibe of this house and this woman bearing down on her spirit in a dazzle of awkwardness. "Uh, yes, the kids decided on buying a variety of puzzle books for the veterans. Where should I put them?" She would gladly be rid of the burden and be on her way.

Connie pointed toward an empty chair next to the china cabinet. "Right there is fine." While Erin unloaded, her friend continued. "The veterans love it when we put puzzle books in our gift bags, and it looks like the C.A.R.'s contributed a good number of them."

Almost against her will, Erin took up the conversation, although her words seemed as artificial as the ingredients in her son's favorite toaster pastries. "I took Ethan and two other members to the dollar store, and they each had ten dollars to spend, so we ended up with thirty."

Connie frowned. "There seem to be a lot more than thirty."

"I kicked in a few more."

"Very nice. Amanda and I will distribute the bags at the VA."

Erin couldn't think of another thing to say, not after what had happened. She wouldn't have stepped foot in this house had she not been responsible for the George Taylor Society, Children of the American Revolution's contribution.

"Do you have time for a cup of tea?"

Erin's back stiffened. She glanced toward the front door.

"Please." Connie pressed her right hand to her chest. "I'm desperate to talk to you."

She looked into her friend's eyes for the first time since arriving and noticed under the flawless hair and makeup, the woman's eyes swelled with tears, highlighting dark smudges. She obviously hadn't slept well.

Her head tingled as Erin allowed herself to follow Connie into the kitchen where two years earlier, she'd met Paul during Easton Heritage Day. A caramel-scented candle burned on the granite-topped island. How often she'd sat there since moving back to her hometown, over light-hearted conversations, thanking God that although she'd left her best friend Melissa in Lansdale, she'd found another kindred spirit. At least until now.

Connie chattered about nothing in particular as she busied herself with tea preparation while Erin stewed in her own juices, as her Grammy Ott used to say. She'd never been much for small talk, and certainly, under the circumstances, she had nothing to contribute. Fortunately, Connie didn't seem to expect anything. The tea kettle finally announced the completion of its job, and Connie tipped the boiling water into two Limoges mugs with Earl Grey tea bags. She placed sugar and cream, along with two gleaming teaspoons onto the table. Normally she offered a selection of cookies from a favorite Easton bakery, but Erin didn't mind the oversight. She'd never be able to choke one down today.

They went about fixing their tea as they liked the brew, placing the spent bags on tiny holders in the shape of autumn leaves. After sipping from the mug, Connie spoke first, reaching across the table and covering Erin's hand with her own.

"I feel just awful about what's happened, but I want you to know I had absolutely nothing to do with it."

Erin raised an eyebrow, wanting to pull away but allowing her hand to rest under the warm covering. All she knew was what Paul had told her, and as he'd emphasized, that was second-hand, information which they examined from every conceivable angle until they exhausted themselves of the topic.

"I'm amazed you would even be talking to me, let alone sitting here now."

Erin slid her hand back and cupped the mug. "What I heard was pretty bad."

"Maybe we could start with that, then I'll tell you what happened."

"All right then." Erin took a deep breath. "While I was in Atlanta with Derek, promoting the new

4

book, there was a special meeting of the Kichline Center board, which seems to have been timed rather conveniently."

Connie nodded, wincing.

"At the meeting, Craig Reldan said he didn't think I should be the director, because I haven't overseen the renovation, and because I'm too busy with my book writing." She paused, seeing Connie closing her eyes as if against a blow, nodding. "He said you wanted to replace me because you're the one doing the hands-on work." She sipped her tea to wash down the lump in her throat, allowing Connie an opportunity to respond.

"You're correct about him calling a meeting, and I also believe he timed it to coincide with your being out of town. I suggested we wait until you returned, but he said there was an urgent matter we needed to discuss. When I offered to set up a Zoom meeting so you could participate, he refused." She sighed, staring into her mug. "At the meeting he said pretty much what you just said. He didn't think your being director was appropriate."

"How did everyone respond?" She wanted to know who'd been on her side.

"There were arguments back and forth, but Craig dominated the discussion and badgered everyone to see things his way. You know how he is—used to getting what he wants, especially because his foundation is funding a large chunk of the renovations. When someone, I forget who, asked what he suggested, he said I should be the director." She began gesturing with her hands. "Well, I just jumped out of my seat and said there was no way, that this was your assignment, your family's heritage, not mine, and you had been appointed to the job. We couldn't just change horses in midstream."

The ice in Erin's spirit toward Connie began to melt, but she still felt glacial about Craig Reldan, whom she'd never particularly cared for. A prominent Easton businessman and philanthropist who wore tailored shirts and a Rolex, he carried himself as if he owned the place, and everyone in it. Some said the latter was true of more than a few people.

"He wanted to put a motion to a vote, but I and two others told him we couldn't, that it wasn't our place. The board and the director functioned under the auspices of Lafayette's president and the history department, and they needed to be brought into the discussion. I knew stalling would give us more time to deal with this nonsense. And that's how it ended, with Craig vowing to contact the college's overseers before meeting again to vote."

Erin heard a thump on the front porch, then a delivery van pulling away. Her heart pounding she said, "Thank you for defending me. This is better, and worse, than I thought." When Connie raised an eyebrow, Erin explained. "Better because you defended me, and we can be our friendly selves again." She offered a smile as a kind of salve to the cut they'd sustained. "Worse because Craig is going through with his plan. What does he have against me? I've never crossed him and hardly know him."

Connie was sitting taller, and even the dark circles under her eyes appeared to be retreating. "I suspect part of it is jealousy because of your heritage, while he's a relative newbie, and the other is resentment. He likes to control what's happening in Easton's cultural life, and he felt out of joint because the Kichline Center was created without his input. He realizes you're not someone he can easily control."

She pressed her lips together, absorbing the information. Once again, she felt Connie's hand over hers, the cocoa eyes wide, brimming.

"Please say you believe me, Erin. I hate this thing between us."

She found her voice. "I believe you."

"Hey, Mom, the food truck is here!" Ethan's voice blended with the howling of their basset hound.

Erin finished washing her hands at the powder room sink, dried them on the towel one of her guys had dropped onto the floor, and hung the damp object properly on the rack. "Okay, I'm coming! Did you open the garage door?"

"Yeah. He's just opening the back of the truck."

She watched as Ethan put his backpack on the family room sofa and reached down to pet Toby behind the ears. "How was school?"

The eleven-year-old shrugged. "Fine."

Toby's rear right leg thumped, and he raised his jowly face in ecstasy.

"Did you pass your history test?"

He grinned. "Yup. Got a ninety-six."

"You better, or I'm not really your mother." She mussed his hair, happy to be feeling a bit lighter after the visit with Connie, although the guilt over having mistrusted her lingered like a bad smell.

"Mom, is it true you're not going to be the boss at the Kichline Center?"

She caught her breath. "Where did you hear that?"

"Some kid asked me at school."

"What kid?" She wondered what kid in the world would know anything about this.

"Some dork. He's always bragging." He twisted his mouth, then spat out, "His name's Finn Reldan."

Erin closed her eyes and exhaled. *That must be Craig's son, or grandson. I don't really know how old Craig is, but I think he's on a second marriage, so the boy could be either.*

"So Mom, are you getting fired or something?"

Kids could be so blunt. "I don't know exactly, Ethan. Someone doesn't like having me in charge."

"Why?"

"It's complicated."

"I'm a big kid. I understand things, which is why I also need a real cell phone."

She did not need this. Not now. Not ever. This unceasing litany designed, she felt sure, to wear her resolve to a nub. A hard knock at the door leading to the garage gave her a reprieve, however temporary.

"The groceries are here. Give me a hand."

Normally, she got Ethan to set the table, but tonight she wanted as much solitude as she could grab to process what was happening. Her life used to be so stable, so routine, so ... she allowed herself a smile ... so predictable. She could not bring herself to think "boring," but the idea hovered around the edges of her thoughts. She had taught part time at Hatfield College, finding a comfortable niche with the same three American history courses she offered to international, mostly Korean, students. In her neighborhood, a Lansdale cul-de-sac, mostly genial families gathered for Easter Egg Hunts, trick or treating, and summer block parties. Even Toby had his favorites among the resident dogs, if not the cats. She loved her life, cherished her husband, enjoyed having his parents living two blocks away, near her best friend Melissa.

Then in one fell swoop, like Job, she found herself sitting among the ashes of her life trying to find relief from the devastation of Jim's sudden, brief bout with cancer. She found herself a widow, and a single mother. The crowning insult was losing her job after the college passed her over for a promotion because she hadn't completed her doctoral dissertation.

In the past two years, she'd completed her degree and accepted a position at her alma mater, Lafayette, and moved back to her hometown after nearly three decades away, to the very house a favorite aunt had owned. This was a season in which she was reconnecting with her family as well as her birthplace, yet the times also contained a heaping serving of sadness. Her father had recently died, after his second wife passed the previous year, and Erin's mother was losing what little eyesight she had left. Ethan hadn't adjusted as well as they'd hoped initially, although he was finding his way performing in school plays.

Some part of her life always seemed in flux since Jim's death, leading her to feel as if she were in a giant game of whack-a-mole. Even the best things, like marrying the handsome, kind-hearted Paul Bassett this past July produced change—and adjustments. So did the traveling she was doing to promote the book she'd just coauthored with renowned historian Derek McCutcheon. Just as she had found herself adapting to those sea changes, here she was, caught in yet another vortex. Her mind went into its most recent default mode, gnawing at the problem.

If I'm not the director of the Kichline Center, Herman Weinreich will have no leverage with his superiors to keep me on the college's payroll, unless he offers me an adjunct teaching position. She sniffed. *Been there, done that. Don't want to do it again. I have so looked forward to heading up the Center, to sharing Easton's colonial history in the place my ancestors lived.* Her thoughts shifted in a different direction. *I would probably stay on the board, or would I? Even if I did, what kind of relationships would I be able to have with people who backstabbed me?* Her stomach churned, and her thoughts whiplashed from one problem to the next. *If I lose that position, I'll also lose Ethan's college tuition benefit and health insurance. But then again, Paul is building up his list of law clients, Ethan might not even want to go to Lafayette, and I am writing books with Derek McCutcheon, which gives us a measure of financial stability.*

Erin glanced down at Toby and said, "What would Grandfather Peter do?" After a moment she spoke again. "He certainly wouldn't fall into a ditch of self-pity. Not him. He'd be happy for all the blessings he'd once had." The thought occurred to her, life hadn't been exactly perfect during her first marriage in those days she now had a tendency to idealize. After all, hadn't she, during those years, distanced herself from her family, avoiding the dysfunction between her divorced parents with all the ugly tentacles wrapping themselves around other relationships? Hadn't she kept Ethan from knowing his grandparents and extended family beyond a passing nod at Christmas and Easter? Hadn't her husband never so much as met her father?

As she began placing napkins to the left of three forks, she breathed a prayer of thanksgiving, including the way God had already used, and would continue to use, any stressful things for her good and his glory. Then came the sound of the garage door opening, and Toby's nails clicking on the floor in his pursuit of Paul, his new best friend. *That dog is in need of a groomer's appointment. I'll try to call tomorrow.* Her husband bounded into the family room after slamming the door behind him, a habit she found jarring. There was no time to ponder this idiosyncrasy, however, when he enfolded her in a bear hug and planted a solid kiss on her lips. Considering how they'd parted in the morning with the gravest of expressions over the Kichline Center situation, she wondered what had brought about such a transformation.

"You're never going to believe what happened today." His face was a flashlight, beaming all over the room.

"Whatever it is, I can top it." She knew she couldn't, but gladness brought out the banter in her.

"I sincerely doubt that."

She lifted her chin and folded her arms across her chest. "Connie Pierce's Christmas shopping is not only done, but all her presents are wrapped."

Paul sniffed. "Is that all you got?" He broke into a sixty-watt smile. "Connie Schmonnie. Christmas has just come for you."

Erin drew back her head, lips pressed together. "What's going on?" For the first time, she realized Paul was holding something behind his back.

"You may not remember, but I had an appointment at four today with Jarvis Zendowski. He's the historian the church hired to sort through the archives."

She did recall how the consistory had voted to engage the man to find out exactly what was in the church's historical collections. People called the office regularly asking for genealogical information, and besides, Pastor Stan wanted to put together a small exhibit in one of the alcoves featuring artifacts from First Church's past. A grant from the Reldan Foundation was paying for the project, probably Erin thought, as a guilt offering from Craig, who seemed to think his contributions more than made up for never darkening the church door.

"Well, Jarvis discovered something you just have to see, and Pastor Stan wanted you to have dibs.

Put these on first." He handed her a pair of white gloves, and as she slipped them on, wondered what in the world was going on. Then Paul made a grand show of sliding into her range of vision an object wrapped tightly in a copy of *The Express Times*.

She reached for the package, which felt like a thin book. "What is it?" Her heart drummed in her chest.

"Open it." Her dark-blond-haired husband's eyes shone like an eager schoolboy's.

Erin peeled back the paper and found inside a faded brown-leather volume. She stared first at the wordless cover, then upon opening it, clutched the book to keep herself from dropping it: "Peter Kichline, esq., Easton, Penna. 1781."

CHAPTER TWO

"I am the resurrection and the life, saith the Lord; he that believeth in me, though he were dead, yet shall he live: and whosoever liveth and believeth in me shall never die."

Peter Kichline stood at his brother's grave absorbing the ancient words of comfort, on ground Andrew had donated to his church decades earlier.

The burly young pastor continued, a man born in this country but employing the tongue of his fathers. "None of us liveth to himself, and no man dieth to himself; for whether we live, we live unto the Lord, and whether we die, we die unto the Lord: whether we live therefore or die, we are the Lord's."

Next to the plot where Andrew would be lowered into the ground lay his first wife, Catherine Susanna, who'd preceded him in death just four years ago. Peter had also buried a wife, two to be exact, Margaretta in 1766, Anna in 1773. He had come pretty close to death himself three years later on a brutally hot summer day on Brooklyn's Gowanus Heights when a Hessian had driven a bayonet into Peter's left arm. During the first months of his captivity, Peter had faced a different fight, to overcome a raging infection. And yet, he had been spared.

A verse from Psalm 139 surfaced while a soft breeze tickled his cheek: "And in Your book were written all the days that were ordained for me, when as yet there was not one of them." Something in his spirit moved the stone of grief from this open tomb to admit a momentary joy at the thought of being hemmed in, behind and before by a loving, purposeful God. Every day ordained. Every day precious.

The pastor continued the liturgy. "Oh death, where is thy sting? Oh grave, where is thy victory? Thanks be to God, which giveth us the victory through our Lord Jesus Christ! Amen."

"Amen." His voice mingled with the other mourners. Victory over death itself. He marveled over the concept as if he'd just heard about it for the very first time and yet, where else than at a freshly dug grave would these words impart the greatest impact? Above their heads even the leaves bore glorious witness to a life well-lived, and a life yet to come.

Peter didn't often think about such things—a man with little patience for navel gazing—but there was no getting around the reality of being in the autumn of his own life. Some might even say at nearly fifty-nine, he was in a headlong rush toward old age. His sandy hair had faded to an ashy gray, and when dampness, rain, or a deep freeze settled over the village of Easton, his various aches and pains came to roost. Aside from a pardonable surge at his waistline, he'd managed to stay fit, possessed all his own teeth, and despite a need for spectacles to read, his eyesight was still keen. His wife Catherine had more than once pronounced him distinguished.

Truly, his immediate family attested to his one foot in youth and the other in advancing age. At his side, his seven-year-old daughter Elizabeth leaned into him while next to her, twenty-one-year-old Susannah held her stepsister's hand. Peter was still coming to terms with Susanna's being Mrs. Peter Snyder for a year now. Whatever doubts he'd harbored about his former indentured servant had imploded under the weight of the young man's unbridled devotion to the Kichline family and its eldest daughter. Peter's heart filled at the way Snyder had conveyed Peter's immediate family to be with him at the burial today. A man needed such comfort after passing through those last days with Andrew and now, the letting go of one so dear. His mind wandered back to the urgent summons, a few days earlier ...

"Peter, you're pale as a ghost. What is wrong?"

The letter with his brother Charles's blocky handwriting went limp in Peter's right hand. "My brother Andrew's heart is weak. Charles is urging me to come to Bedminster if I want to see him again before ..."

Catherine put her hand on his arm, steadying him. "Oh my dearest! You must go right away." She flew into action. "Bett and I will pack your clothes, and Joe can ready your horse. You needn't concern yourself with a single detail."

He nodded his head, mute, picturing Andrew clinging to what was left of his time.

Peter's family had him on the road within an hour of receiving the summons, which had been posted three days earlier. As he followed the river road to the Kichline homestead for the next six hours, he continually fended off an assailing concern of being too late. At the end of the journey, however, a different kind of surprise awaited him. Andrew was sitting up in bed, smiling.

"As you can see," the youngest of the brothers said, "I am still very much alive."

Peter had sunk into the chair next to Andrew's bed as if he'd just been paroled from a different kind of prison than he'd known in New York. His voice was hoarse. "Thanks be to God."

They had talked for an hour before Andrew's second wife, whose name was also Catherine, entered and with a single look, dispersed the meeting. Outside the sick room, Peter engaged her in conversation, while they walked to the parlor in the candlelit twilight.

"He seems completely recovered."

"I have thought so myself." Catherine's eyes said otherwise.

He sat in a chair she waved him toward. "Something tells me you aren't so sure."

"He hasn't been able to be out of bed for more than a few minutes at a time. He's become quite weak since the episode." She clasped her trembling hands upon her lap.

"How did all of this come upon him?"

"He was helping split kindling for your mother because he saw the woodpile was getting low, and Abraham just happened to be coming for the same reason, to help his grandmother. Abraham says Andrew insisted upon doing the work. You see, your brother has been unusually tired recently, and his color has been, well, off. But you know Andrew." She closed her eyes, sighing. "All Abraham could do was pile the wood as Andrew did the splitting. And then, quite suddenly, Andrew clutched his chest and went down." She shuddered, unable to continue for a few moments. "The next thing I knew, Abraham had summoned your brother Charles and the doctor, who said we should prepare ourselves for the worst, that Andrew's heart had given out."

Peter felt a need to stay quiet while she gathered her thoughts. "Has he had any heart trouble before this?"

"Looking back over the last year, I see signs of illness. I think his latest service as Sub-lieutenant of the County drained him." She looked up at Peter. "You understand, don't you?"

"Yes, I most certainly do." He thought back over his own term as Lieutenant of Northampton County.

Catherine continued. "Not two days later, Andrew was awake and alert, and asking Charles and Abraham to help him write his last will and testament."

His eyebrows raised. "And did he complete the task?"

Catherine nodded her head, sighing. "Yes. This is what puzzles me. He behaves as if he's recovering, but then he insists upon making a will. Does this make sense to you?"

Peter pressed his lips together and, after a few moments of consideration, said, "Yes, I believe so. He wants to make sure you and the younger children are provided for, just in case."

For the next two days, the possibility of Andrew's demise faded, prompting their mother's optimistic assessment, "He appears to be out of the woods." Peter decided to stay another day to linger with him and the rest of the family, since he so seldom got to enjoy their extended company. Although Peter couldn't be completely sure, an educated hunch told him the end of the wearying war was a distinct prospect, and when that happy day arrived, he would be free to gather with these treasured people more frequently.

On the third day of his visit, Peter went into Andrew's room to beg a game of backgammon, hoping to take a short walk in the cooling outdoors, but his brother's current appearance surprised him as much as the initial visit, though not in the same direction. This time, Andrew had taken a different kind of turn, an unmistakably otherworldly one. Never before had Peter seen such a gentle, even submissive, look on his brother's face, adjectives no one who knew Andrew would have ever used to describe him. He gazed toward the back of the room, past Peter. Catherine entered, her own eyes widening, her hand flying to her mouth. Peter leaned over his brother. "Andrew. Are you ready for that game we talked about?"

The lips smiled. "I am otherwise engaged, Peter. Someone else is calling for me." He lifted his right hand, which seconds later fell to the covers.

... The young minister's voice came back into focus, and Peter bowed his head at the invitation to pray. "Almighty God, with whom do live the spirits of those who depart hence in the Lord, and with whom the souls of the faithful, after they are delivered from the burden of the flesh, are in joy and felicity, we give Thee hearty thanks for the good examples of those Thy servants who, having finished their course in faith, now do rest from their labors ..."

Comforting words, familiar words Peter first heard as a rough and tumble boy of six back in Kircheim, though he didn't fully understand their meaning then. Just that life had changed quite suddenly when his father died, leaving behind Peter, his pregnant mother, and little Charles, Karl, as they'd called him in the old country. Johann Andreas Kichline of Switzerland, late of Germany, had died on September 23rd in the year 1728 before his namesake could even be held in his father's arms. Little Andreas, or Andrew, first saw daylight on December 15th. All these years later, Andrew had passed away on September 22nd, united with his father in death as they had not had the pleasure in life.

Peter looked over at his eighty-year-old mother, still standing strong, though slightly stooped in the shoulders, a recent widow herself after burying her second husband. Peter and Charles had grown up under the guidance of a firm, affectionate mother and Michael Koppelger. Peter had never been able to think of him as a father, although he respected the man and had even developed affection for him. Perhaps, he thought, Charles's and Andrew's connection to him had gone to a deeper level because they'd never known their birth parent. This might have also been why they had stayed in Bedminister after the family emigrated to America in 1742, while Peter had soon gone off to shift for himself.

All three of them had built lives on the foundation of family, faith, and service, Peter and Andrew, men of action, leaders in their respective communities, colonels in the War for Independence, and in the dramatic buildup of the prior years. Peter had always been more of a diplomat and statesman than Andrew, who spoke his mind, often without first considering what was passing across his lips. He'd been all, "ready, fire, aim," ruffling several flocks of feathers during his life. Charles, on the other hand, was the most soft-spoken of the three, a man of deep intellect and deliberation who took his time weighing various options. He hadn't even married until he turned thirty-nine. No one would exactly think of him as a short man, but next to his six-feet-plus brothers, Charles always appeared smaller, if not consequential, a mistake others quickly corrected as they got to know him better.

Charles stood around five-ten, and his waist coat had always tugged a little tighter. Compared to his brothers, Charles didn't seem as imposing or even illustrious, but he was in his own way a force to be reckoned with.

Peter looked beyond his family, immediate as well as extended, pleasantly surprised to see Phoebe Benner Hanson, the niece of Andrew's first wife, and her pastor husband. Their eyes met, and they exchanged a silent, respectful smile. There were many other mourners outside the family circle, filling the cemetery courtyard all the way to the stone fence, dozens, perhaps up to a hundred of them. Peter's spirit swelled to realize whatever ill feelings Andrew might have caused in his life, he had clearly created a good deal more affection and respect.

Peter found himself staring down the span of his own eventful life. Like Andrew, he had older children, now independent, as well as much younger ones. At thirty-one, Peter Junior lived with his wife in Easton when he wasn't serving in the army, building up a fulling business. Twenty-eight-year-old Andrew had, like his sister Susanna, married the previous year and, with his slightly younger brother Jacob, oversaw their father's saw and grist mills along the Bushkill Creek. Then there was little Elizabeth, sister to a baby brother who'd died three years ago. Peter ran a finger under his cravat where sweat puddled in the warmth of the Indian Summer day. Close by, bees swarmed for the last of the nectar from flowers clinging to what was left of their glory. Were these also his latter days?

Would his own wife and children be throwing dirt on him any time soon?

He shook himself free of the intrusive thoughts, choosing instead to focus on the dark-haired minister, who was drawing the graveside service to a close. For the first time, Peter noticed an unmistakably Mennonite couple in their distinctive plain dress standing several yards beyond the last row of mourners. He wondered if they might be part of the graveside tableau, or if they'd wandered into the scenario and stopped for a look. But no. They were paying too close attention, their postures oriented toward the service, to be casual observers. Yes, and there was the young woman dabbing at her eyes. He wondered what their connection was to his brother, and why they were standing so far off.

Younger family members assisted the older ones from the graveside to Andrew's house just across from the church to a feast the ladies of the congregation and neighborhood had prepared. Peter had caught a glimpse of the spread just before the funeral, smiling to himself at how much Andrew would have enjoyed all the aromatic, tasty offerings. He found for the first time in two days his mouth actually watered at the thought of the Pennsylvania German delights awaiting him, but something inside compelled him to greet those Mennonites first, especially since the other mourners had passed by them without acknowledgment.

"Are you coming, husband?" Catherine asked.

"Yes, my dear, but I must greet someone first. You go on ahead of me with Elizabeth. I'll join you at the house."

The little girl opened her mouth, but her mother spoke first. "Come along, Lizzy. There's something inside I especially want to show you."

Peter gave his child a reassuring pat on the shoulder, realizing how clingy she'd been since Andrew's death. Perhaps Elizabeth harbored her own fears about her aging father, fears he wanted to head off at the pass. "I'll be there before you even have a chance to miss me."

"Come along." Catherine took their daughter's hand and led her to the house, fading into the flow of mourners.

He strode in the direction of the reclusive couple, who stood statue still, in the drama, but not of it. When Peter introduced himself, they did a simultaneous imitation of startled rabbits.

"I want to thank you for coming to my brother's service."

The woman's mouth had opened, but nothing came out. Her husband gave a terse nod, which Peter took for a response.

"May I ask how you knew him?"

The wife turned quickly to her husband, who stared in the direction of the grave. He seemed in no hurry to respond and for a moment, Peter wondered, judging by their tense posture, if they might just turn and flee. The only sound came from the low chatter of family and friends in the background. He had a sudden realization of what might be happening, based on his own prior experience with Mennonites and Moravians, each of them pacifists at a time when their beliefs clashed with the needs of colonies striving for independence from Great Britain.

After some moments the man said, "Your brother was good to us, brought my parents wood when they were sick, and we were away. We wanted to pay our respects. We are sorry for your loss."

Peter realized he would get no further information from them. "I am pleased to hear he was good to you. We are gathering at his home for a meal. Will you join us?"

"We cannot, but I thank you just the same." The man raised the brim of his hat about an inch, turned to his wife, and they walked in the opposite direction.

Peter watched until they faded into a sun-splashed copse of trees.

CHAPTER THREE

Erin hadn't leaped like this since junior high cheerleading tryouts, then she broke into a dance worthy of Shakira while simultaneously bursting into tears. Toby followed by rearing back his head and letting loose a howl. "Is this what I think it is?" she cried over the din.

Paul hushed the dog, who ceased and desisted. Her husband wore the expression of the proverbial cat who'd swallowed a particularly savory mouse. "What do you think it is?"

The words caught in the back of her throat. Then she blurted, "This belonged to my Grandfather Peter."

"Yes, love, this belonged to the Colonel. It's his journal."

Her hands shaking, she turned the first page which revealed a short, elegant handwriting, quite faded but still discernable. She tried making out a date, but her moist eyes prevented her from focusing. She wanted nothing more than to take this treasure into her home office and read until the end. "And you found this in the church's archives?"

"Yes. There are some cabinets and standing closets in a back room, and Jarvis has been pouring through and over them. The church's entire history is contained there, including some of the first printed bulletins, sermons from the early 19th century, boxes of vital statistic-type records—marriages, births, baptism, deaths, church officers, you name it."

Erin shivered to consider those objects, more precious to her than much fine gold, wishing she were right there next to this Jarvis fellow as he combed through them. But first, there was the matter of this incredible journal.

"Where did you find this?"

"Tucked inside an ancient, yellowing envelope with no name, no address, no markings, no nothing. Apparently someone a long time ago thought giving this diary to the church would be a good way to preserve it."

She tilted her head, feeling the happy weight of the book in her trembling hands. "So, you don't have any idea who had it?"

"Generations of Kichlines, right down to you and your mother, have belonged to the church, and I think somewhere along the way, maybe a hundred years or more ago judging by the design of the envelope we found the book in, someone found this in an attic or basement and had the wherewithal to give it to the church for safekeeping."

Perhaps one of her ancestors. "Why the church? Why not the historical society?"

"Who knows?" Paul lifted his hands, palms upward. "They were probably more closely connected to the church."

Just then Ethan padded into the family room in his sock feet, looking first at his mom, then at Paul. "Hey. What's going on?"

Paul glanced at Erin. "Did you start supper?"

"I got as far as setting the table, if that counts."

"And that's as far as you'll be getting tonight. We're doing take-out tonight. Ethan, get your shoes on. We'll go pick up some food. Your mom has something more important to do than cooking."

"Work?" Ethan asked.

Paul ruffled the boy's hair. "Nope. A labor of love."

She arranged herself in her office recliner, placed a cozy throw over her lap, and breathed a prayer of thanks to the Giver of all good gifts. Then she opened the cover to venture inside the Xanadu of her ancestor's world, in his own words. Erin breathed a sigh upon discovering the binding held firmly; she had thirty-year-old paperbacks in far worse shape, but then they hadn't been manufactured with nearly as much craftsmanship. She pictured a printing shop on old Northampton Street, or perhaps Main Street in Bethlehem, maybe even Ben Franklin's print shop in Philadelphia, as the source of this journal. As far as she knew, there hadn't been such a place in 18th century Easton that far back, narrowing the possibilities.

The leather edges showed signs of wear, as if mice might have enjoyed a nibble in some long ago garret, and the edges of the pages were no longer uniform, but soft with touch.

Whoever its keeper had been over the years had treated the journal well, or at least kept the book from fire, flood, and plague. Its years of largely undisturbed residence in the church vault had no doubt contributed to its overall state.

Toby wandered into the office and fixed a baleful expression on her. She'd never known a basset hound to prefer a human lap to a monogrammed dog bed, but this one did.

"Not today, old boy. I can't run the risk of you drooling over this gem." She pointed with a gloved finger.

The dog sauntered over to his appointed place and laid his head on his forepaws.

Prior to this astonishing find, Erin had seen up close and personal Peter Kichline, Sr.'s handwriting on deeds and other legal documents, including his parole statement from the war. Through these, and various articles and papers others had written about him across the centuries, she had developed an emotional connection to her extraordinary relative. Never, however, had she been this close to knowing the thoughts and intentions of his own heart, as well as his keen mind.

Her mouth watering, as if she were about to indulge in the greatest of fare, she put on her reading glasses, took a deep breath, and opened to the first of what appeared to be no more than a few dozen pages. Her approach needed to be just right as she opened the door to her ancestor's everyday life. Would she go through all the rooms at once, as if on a guided tour, or take her time in each one before moving to the next? She certainly wouldn't casually flip through as if this were a Talbots catalogue. She decided to turn a few of the pages to get a general lay of the landscape, joy clutching at her with the appearance of his neat script. "Wow!" Toby raised his head an inch. "Wow! Wow! Wow!" Just as suddenly, she groaned. "This was written in German." She peered more closely. "He seems to have gone back and forth between English and German, heavy on the German, but then wouldn't a person use his native language in a journal?"

She was no slouch with German, but neither was she fluent. Coupled with the fading ink, reading her ancestor's journal was not going to be the work of a single sitting.

"Okay, okay, let's start at the beginning. She turned back to the first page.

Bedminster, Penna., September 26, 1781. Heute haben wir Andrew begraben."

"Andrew and Bedminster I understand. Let's see, 'heute.' 'Heute.' Ah, right, 'today.' So, 'Today have we Andrew.' What is 'begraben?'" She entered the word into an online translator, which came up "buried." "Okay, then, 'Today we buried Andrew.' Oh, that is sad! I wonder if this was his brother Andrew, my many times great uncle." She frowned, accessing her memory to climb her family tree. "Bedminster isn't too far from Easton." She picked up her phone and did a distance check. "About twenty-three miles," she said aloud. "That's where Grandfather Peter's two brothers, Charles and Andrew, and their mother, lived, so let's find out if that date corresponds with that particular Andrew's death. She knew the family tended to use the same names over and over through the generations."

Erin carefully placed the journal on her end table, reached for the laptop at the side of her desk, and slid it over to herself. A few moments later she was on Ancestry.com looking up "Andrew Kichline." At first, she came up lemons, but when she typed in his German name, Johann Andreas Kichline, there he was, Peter and Charles's brother. "Okay, so Grandfather Peter is referring to his brother Andrew in this entry, and he died on September 22, 1781. That's definitely him."

She scanned the diary, eager to know what Peter had to say about the passing of his younger brother.

Johann Andreas Koechlein – Geboren 15 Dec. 1728 – Gestorben 22 Sept 1781

Erin straightened in the chair. "Born and died." She switched back to the family tree to find out where Andrew fit in. "Let's see, he was six years younger than Peter and two years younger than Charles. How old was he when he died? Wow, only fifty-two!" Suddenly, the early fifties didn't seem the prehistoric times she considered them just a few years ago. At nearly fifty herself, Erin shivered. "I wonder what the cause of his death was." Another matter occurred to her. "If I'm not mistaken, didn't he bury his wife not too long before that?" She referred back to Ancestry and saw Catherine Benner Kichline had indeed passed away in 1777, but her great uncle had remarried, interestingly a woman with the same first name.

At the end of twenty minutes, she had managed to translate the unruled first page of the diary and sat back chewing on a number two pencil.

Andreas was born in Kircheim, Bolanden three months following the death of our father, Johann Andreas Koechlein. Our mother, Anna Margaretha Hahn, wife of Michael Koppelger, now deceased, emigrated with us to America in 1742.

Andrew married Catherine Susanna Benner. Children: Abraham, Andrew, Jacob, Elizabeth, John, Susanna, Peter. Children by his second wife are Sarah and one unborn. All were present at their father's service, in the church and at the grave.

Erin had visited her many times great uncle Andrew's grave two years ago and now imagined herself present at the time of his death, a tear slipping down her cheek because he'd never known his last child.

A large number of people came from the community, including those who sometimes were at odds with Andrew. Somehow he must have made amends with them. Standing at the edge of the cemetery, quite by themselves, was a youthful Mennonite couple. When I greeted them afterwards, they indicated Andrew had shown them kindness, but they would say no more. Only my mother and brother Charles nodded toward them from a distance. What is their story? When a life ends is a good time to bury ill will. Perhaps these people and their presence are indications of healing. This is good, for the war has taken a toll.

Following a double space, at the bottom of the page Erin read:

Andrew was an honorable, upright man. He shall be missed. May he rest in God.

"Oh, Erin, what a find! And you get to keep the journal?"

She put a mug of Yorkshire tea with all the fixings on her side table, and lay the cell phone next to it, tapping the "speaker" function. "Not exactly, Melissa. The decision hasn't been made yet about where it will go."

"Don't you wish you could keep it?"

Erin sighed. "Part of me does, but as a historian, I want to share this with others, and besides, I'm not the only Kichline around these parts."

"Maybe it will find a permanent home at the Kichline Center."

"Maybe." She didn't want the conversation to veer off in that direction. Not now. Melissa didn't know what had happened, and Erin wanted to save the telling for another time. She needed to focus on something happy.

"I always think a diary is the most exciting thing to read years later. Did you keep one when you were growing up?"

"Yes. My parents gave me a little green one with a tiny lock for Christmas when I was oh, maybe seven." She dated everything from their divorce, and since Audrey and Tony were still together, Erin figured she was seven or eight at the time. "How about you?"

Her best friend laughed. "Oh, yes, I had one just like you're describing, except mine was light blue.

I had no idea what you were supposed to write in a diary, and when my mother gave me an old box with my things in it a few years ago, I found it, still locked, and no key."

Erin laughed. "What did you do?"

"I picked the lock with a bobby pin, a trick my brother perfected when we were kids. Did your brother ever pick your diary lock?"

"I hope not."

"Well, mine did, and he ran around the house hooting and hollering, reading my pathetic entries at the top of his lungs for his little buddies to hear."

Erin could hear the wincing in Melissa's voice.

"All of that came back when I opened the diary a few years ago. Do you know what I wrote?"

She had no idea.

"'I love Scott Baio.' Over and over again. What kind of little mind does that?"

She burst out laughing, "I'll tell you, Melissa. While you were writing about your undying love for Scott Baio, I was pledging mine to John Travolta."

An earsplitting howl came through the phone. Then her friend went off on one of her tangents. "My oldest brother was so big on John Travlota. You should've seen him going to the prom. White tux, black shirt, the whole enchilada. I used to catch him dancing to the 'Saturday Night Fever' soundtrack in our basement, perfecting his moves. As for his date ..."

"Uh, Melissa?"

"I've done it again, haven't I?"

Erin sipped her tea then said, "Yep."

"So sorry. Back to your grandfather's diary. "How much have you translated?"

"Just the first page. The writing is faded, and much is in German, which slows me down. I can't wait to get back and read more, but I also couldn't wait to tell you about the find."

"Thank you. I appreciate that. Actually, I'd love to see the diary. How's about I come up to Easton? What's your schedule like?"

Erin groaned to herself but said, "I'll figure something out. I'd love to see you."

She could do this blindfolded. Bakery and bananas, aisle one. Tuna and small cans of pop top beans—heaven forbid Erin put the fifteen-ounce ones in the cart —aisle three. Toiletries, aisle four, frozen dinners and ice cream, aisles ten and eleven, followed by juice and soda, paper goods and dairy. In truth, she could recite the Stauffer's mac and cheese dinner's sku right along with the Pledge of Allegiance. Yet, each time Audrey came to the independent grocery on Memorial Parkway, she moved at the pace of Friday rush hour traffic, peering into the shelves as if she were searching for the lost island of Atlantis. Erin could get the shopping done in a quarter of the time, and when she offered to do so, she received the full contents of Audrey's wrath. The sight of her mother smoldering had closed and locked that subject from now until doomsday.

Erin checked her watch as her mother pushed the laden cart up to the deli counter; they had crossed off half the list (that never changed) in thirty minutes. She closed her eyes and pictured herself sitting at her desk writing one of the final chapters in her second book with Derek McCutchen, about unsung women of the American Revolution. This was far more pleasant than chewing the bitter cud of what was happening at the Kichline Center, something she had kept from her mother. Knowing Audrey, she would march right into Craig Reldan's upmarket office on Northampton Street and demand justice for her maligned daughter. Clearing her mind, Erin focused instead on the box in her trunk containing a certain book she simply could not wait to show her mother, if only this interminable grocery run would end.

The deli clerk broke into a big smile. "Well, hello, Audrey!"

"Hello. Is that Peggy?"

"It sure is. This is your daughter, right?" The sixty-something woman gave Erin a thorough once-over.

Audrey beamed. "Yes, this is my daughter, Erin Miles, who's a professor and an author. She works on books with Dietrich McAllister."

Erin closed her eyes and shook her head. The deli worker's eyebrows raised. 'Well, that's pretty impressive. What can I get for you today, Audrey—ham salad or chicken salad?"

"The usual."

"Ham salad it is."

In a flash of insight, Erin realized why her legally blind mother insisted on going grocery shopping. This wasn't about procuring food and supplies.

"Why am I wearing these gloves?"

Erin sat beside Audrey on the sofa, ready for the big reveal.

"Because, Mother, I have something amazing to show you."

"Are you wearing gloves too?"

She felt the warmth of her mom's hand covering hers. "Yes, I am."

"So, what is this?"

She removed the ancient book from the box and put the latter beside her. Outside her mother's apartment door the sound of a man and woman talking in the hallway wafted inside. Erin guided her mom's left hand onto the top of the journal.

"It's some kind of book."

"Not just any book. This is Grandfather Peter's diary from 1781!" Her chest swelled.

"No kidding!"

"I kid you not."

"Where did this come from?"

She proceeded to share the story about the find, basking in her mother's delighted astonishment. When she finished, Audrey asked, "Will you read it to me?"

"I must tell you, I've only translated one page so far. It's written mostly in German, and reading the faint writing is slow going."

"Before you do," Audrey said, "just let me touch it again."

The way she caressed their ancestor's diary brought tears to Erin's eyes. Her sentiments exactly.

CHAPTER FOUR

The after-funeral ritual had become too familiar in recent years. Inevitably the dining table groaned under the weight of a copious assortment of redware and pewter bowls, platters, and dishes laden with Pennsylvania German fare—buttered noodles, smoked hams, beef loins, plump chickens, bread the color of coffee, and pickled vegetables of every color and stripe. For dessert, female family and neighbors vied to see who could make the wettest bottom shoo fly pie. The mourners began the repast with respectful murmurs, and as their bellies filled, the mood became more relaxed. There occurred the occasional joke and accompanying laughter about the deceased's newly-endearing foibles.

Peter stood by an open window with his remaining brother appraising the scene, grateful for a touch of fresh air in an increasingly stuffy room.

"She seems to be taking Andrew's death as well as she can." He nodded in the direction of their mother.

Charles swallowed a large piece of pickled beet before answering. "It's never easy to lose a child."

"No. It isn't." The image of his lifeless son Abraham rushed into his mind's eye.

"But you know Mother. She has the long view of life."

"She was like that when Father died all those years ago." He paused, placing his plate on the windowsill and reaching for the tankard of ale. "Do you remember that?"

"Not as well as you do, Peter, but I do recall standing at the graveside with half the village and wondering why we were having church outside."

He cracked a thin smile at the eccentricities of a child's early impressions. "She often said the only thing we can count on is God ..."

His younger brother smiled and finished, "Who never leaves us or forsakes us."

"You do remember, then?" Peter tilted his head.

"That particular verse has been part and parcel of her life since, well, forever."

Charles had always been the most philosophical of the three brothers, and the least physically-oriented. While Andrew and Peter were off fighting during the French and Indian War in their adopted country's dense woods, Charles was sidelined by extreme nearsightedness. During this war for independence, their bookish brother hadn't secured glory on any battlefield, but had faithfully paid the supply tax and provided goods to the Continental Army. A man of high standing in the community, he probably would have been chosen for the Bucks County Committee of Safety, but Peter had long believed Charles had been passed over in favor of the more dynamic Andrew. If the older brother bore any resentment, Peter had never been privy to it.

"I hold close to my heart all of what our dear mother has taught us over the years," Charles was saying.

Peter's chest constricted as he considered the closeness with her he had missed out on as an adult living over twenty miles distance. "I almost envy your position here."

His brother looked up at Peter, his eyes the color of blue mist. "The dashing colonel envies his dumpy brother?"

He gave a short laugh. "You are not dumpy, and I am far from dashing. However, you have enjoyed our dear mother's close company throughout your life."

Charles pursed his lips then said, "And so I have. Do you regret your choice to live in Easton?"

"No." He took a sip of his drink, then placed the pewter vessel next to his plate, a greedy fly quickly nestling on the rim. All those years ago, he'd felt a driving need to strike out on his own, and he had no regrets. "However, even the best choices do not include all we hold dear."

"If you ever put the matter to her, I am certain she would say she understood, and accepted your decision to move elsewhere."

For a few moments they stood in silence, having forgotten their meal, allowing the sound and movement of the packed room to settle upon them. Charles picked up the conversation. "I am happy so many came to pay their respects to Andrew."

Peter read between the lines. "I think when all was said and done, the community realized a man of integrity must make many hard decisions."

"You knew all about that."

He gave a huff.

"You and Andrew were cut from similar cloth, although you wore yours differently."

He grinned, knowing the likeness, as well as the dissimilarities, especially how Andrew tended to speak well in advance of any reflection. Peter considered himself fortunate to have made as few enemies as he had along the path of many decades of public service. He had striven to be as fair as possible, to everyone, regretting those times he had fallen short.

"Tell me, Charles, did you see that young Mennonite couple at the graveside?"

He nodded his head. "Yes. They are the Millers, who have a neighboring farm. I was surprised, though pleased they came."

"This might have to do with the war I suppose?"

"Aaron and Elizabeth are the son and daughter-in-law of Ernst Miller, who has a considerable farm and a thriving blacksmithing business. At least it was. Local patriots pressured him to pay the tax and supply goods to the Cause, but Ernst is a man of outspoken principles. He's also stubborn." He looked at Peter. "You know how Germans can be."

They raised their closed fists to their mouths, sharing a subdued guffaw. "Let me guess; Ernst refused to give what the law required, and officials fined him." A familiar refrain.

"Yes. More than a few in the community boycotted his smithing works as well. Even among the Mennonites, Ernst made enemies of those who believed some cooperation was in order, but he holds to the letter of the law. Some ruffians vandalized his buildings and terrified Mrs. Miller so she was afraid even to go to meeting. Our brother put a stop to the violence, and Aaron, the son, secretly gave what he could without his father's knowledge."

"To comply with the mandates?"

"In part. Aaron, you see, is a closet patriot."

Peter's gray-flecked eyebrows rose. "And our brother Andrew was a closet diplomat?"

"Surprising, but yes."

He took a deep breath, considering this hidden aspect of his brother's boisterous personality. "But the community is unaware of Aaron's support and holds the sins of the father against this next generation."

"Precisely." Charles paused before asking, "Do you think the war might be heading toward a conclusion?"

"If the Battle of the Chesapeake is any indication, I am hopeful the British are getting increasingly into a less tenable position."

"A siege perhaps?"

He nodded his head. "I am thinking along those lines, yes."

"What would we do without the French?"

"They have certainly been our greatest ally." Peter thought back to his meeting with General Lafayette in Bethlehem, following the Battle of Brandywine, then again at Valley Forge.

"After six years, I think we're all frightfully weary of war."

"Amen."

♛

Peter looked up from his pipe and his newspaper as Catherine came through the front door, followed by their daughter-in-law Sarah Doll Kichline. Susannah's head rose from the book she was reading as she sat in the chair nearest her father. Although she was now a married woman with her own home, she often stopped in to spend time with her beloved parent. The women spoke quietly, both of their faces clouded with strain.

"Hello, Peter," Catherine said, entering the parlor. "Hello, Susannah."

"Hello, Mother Catherine."

"Good day, Father Peter, Susannah." Sarah nodded toward them, perfunctory.

"Good day, ladies." He folded and placed the paper on his lap as they came and stood before him, shoulders stooped. "Where have you been that you look so glum?"

They looked at each other, then at him. "To see our Elizabeth," Catherine said.

He frowned. "And how is she coming along?"

"Very slowly."

He looked at Sarah, who had known the loss of a handful of infants through miscarriages and stillbirths. Elizabeth, who had married his son, Andrew, had given birth to a little girl in January, a tiny child who expired in his father's arms on September 8th.

Catherine's voice carried a sigh. "Come, Sarah, let's get a cup of tea."

Peter knew Bett would be only too happy to provide refreshments, but he sensed the women wanted to busy themselves, perhaps with something they could control. He glanced at Susannah, whose face had turned the shade of fireplace ashes. "Dear child! What is the matter?"

She didn't speak for a moment, then seemed to push her words past her teeth. "Papa, there's been so much death. And I'm, I'm afraid ..."

He reached over the table separating them and laid his large hand on her delicate one, hoping to still her trembling. "As you've heard many times, to everything there is a season. This has been our time to mourn."

She looked down into her lap where her forgotten book lay. "Women mourn so very much."

Suddenly he understood, and his heart pounded. "Are you? Are you, then ...?" He didn't think he could bear such news, not now, not yet.

She looked up at him, her chin quivering. "No, Papa, I am not, but lately I think I'd rather never ..."

He spoke to reassure her, despite his own misgivings. "Ah, but think of the joy you would miss." His words seemed to flow some other source. "There's just too much good in life to lose if we let weeping last past the night." He gave into an impulse to remove her from the dour mood that had befallen the room. "Not everything must be difficult." He rose on impulse.

She cracked a smile. "What are you up to, Papa?"

"I have a treat for you. Come with me." He hoped what he wanted to show her was indeed ready to be seen.

The smile widened. "I suppose you are going to take me to Mr. Hart's shop for a peppermint stick?"

"Better than that, but if you still want one, we'll stop there as well."

Peter winked at his daughter as they stood before the door of the little stone schoolhouse at the rear of the German Reformed Church, the first of autumn's fallen leaves blowing gently against their feet. The thumping of footsteps that could only belong to his sturdy, erstwhile quartermaster, neared, and the door thrust open.

"Who ... oh! Colonel Kichline! Mrs. Snyder!" John Spangenberg snapped to attention, then bowed in greeting.

"Good day, Sergeant." Peter pumped the unusually artistic hand seeming out of place in a person with such a substantial frame. "Am I interrupting anything?" He peered around the corner, unsure if school were still in session.

"Please come in. I have just sent the urchins to their respective homes."

Peter wondered how they had missed his daughter Elizabeth.

"I've been expecting you since we spoke last Sunday."

Peter and Susannah entered the fire and lamplit room and followed the teacher down the center aisle to his desk where the tools of his other trade lay scattered.

"Once the children leave, I stay behind for a spell to do my other work. There is, you see, no place and no peace for me once I go home to a house bursting at its seams with my own children." He laughed at his own humor, his cheeks permanently ruddy with mirth, hair a tad windblown, while he attempted to locate some document. "Ah, and here it is!" Suddenly, he appeared nearly shy, clearing his throat, looking down at his feet. "Mrs. Snyder, your father has asked me to present this to you."

Susannah moved her right hand to her breast, glancing first at Peter, then at the schoolmaster before reaching out to accept a marriage *fraktur* from the man with a growing reputation as a folk artist. Beholding her wedding record in vivid colors, with doves, two musicians blowing long horns, and a couple so winsomely crafted, she burst into a great smile.

"Oh, Mr. Spangenberg! Oh! I hardly know what to say." She turned to Peter. "Papa, this is wonderful!"

Warmth spread through his middle and rose to his face. *I am so pleased to have brought her such happiness.*

"Thank you, Papa. Thank you, Mr. Spangenberg. I can hardly wait to show my husband."

"I have already asked William to craft a frame for the wedding record," Peter said. "He will come tomorrow to begin the work. I might have waited until this was completed, but I wanted to show you today."

"And I am so glad you did, that is, show me today."

"I do offer my sincere apologies for having taken so long to complete this."

Peter raised and pushed his hand against the air. "The timing was perfect, Sergeant Spangenberg." He leaned closer to see the joyful document once again, its charm filling his spirit. "You are truly gifted."

A knock sounded at the door, and the teacher called out, "Come in! Ah, Pastor Rodenheimer, please come in."

The minister tipped his hat to Peter and Susannah. "Good day, all. I thought I saw you going into the schoolhouse."

"I am pleased to see you," Peter said.

Susannah curtsied. "Good day, Pastor. Look what Mr. Spangenberg has made for me and my husband."

He walked to the front of the room. "My, but that is fine work. I sometimes feel like breaking into a dance when I behold your art, Mr. Spangenberg. You have a way of capturing joy."

"That is most kind of you, Pastor." Spangenberg gave a small bow.

"Forgive the interruption, but I wonder if I might have a private word with you, Colonel."

"Not at all. Please excuse us." He followed Rodenheimer through the door and outside where the pastor motioned him toward the courtyard.

"Yesterday when the post rider brought the mail, there was a letter for you in my pile." He handed an envelope to Peter.

He frowned. "I'm not sure I understand. Why wasn't this delivered to me directly?"

His shoulders raised, then lowered. "The rider is somewhat new, and rest assured, I have received letters for various Eastonians."

48

"Ah, yes. I do recall getting some of Mr. Traill's correspondence just last week."

He examined the finely woven paper sealed with red wax. Without his spectacles, he couldn't discern its exact representation, but he thought perhaps, it might be a coat of arms. He broke the seal and unfolded the letter, surprised such expensive stationary would contain what appeared to be scrawl. "I do beg your pardon, Pastor, but without my glasses, I find this difficult to read. Will you please do me the honor?"

Rodenheimer accepted the proffered paper, scanning its contents. "This is rather poorly written, in a mixture of German and English. I'll do my best to translate."

> *My der Cl, please meet yr hble servant 2 on the clock, on the 13th Oct. Church in German Valley. Moste irgint.*

CHAPTER FIVE

"When did you say you're going to Chicago?"

"The day after tomorrow."

"I am so proud of you, Erin, collaborating with Derek McCutcheon on a new book and appearing with him on the first one's launch! It's perfect you should be doing one about unsung women of the American Revolution. I would have to pinch myself to make sure I wasn't making it all up."

Her all-time best friend's enthusiasm warmed Erin. "Believe me, sometimes I do."

"Will I be able to watch the Chicago TV event?"

"The book interview will be with a local station, and I can email you the information. Maybe they do livestreaming."

"I got lost in the weeds a week ago trying to find something Ryan told me to watch online. He didn't seem to realize his mom didn't grow up knowing how to navigate cyberspace. First, I went to the organization's Facebook page, and when that didn't work, I tried YouTube, and you wouldn't believe what I found—there are actually recipes that regular people submit with video instructions. I found this really cool one about making Baked Alaska of all things. Have you ever baked Alaska?"

And she's off! Erin sucked in an urge to burst out laughing, not only over Melissa's internet innocence, but her signature way of pursuing conversational rabbit trails. She let her go until Melissa ran out of words, which usually happened about three minutes in.

"Oh, there I go again! Why don't you stop me, Erin? I'm an embarrassment to myself."

"I think you're adorable."

"You're too kind to me. And here you are, getting ready for a huge event, and the meeting over the Kichline Center. Aren't they awfully close to each other?"

Erin took a deep breath. "They just scheduled a board discussion for the night after I get back."

"I'd like to come up there and wring that guy's neck!" She paused. "Better than wringing his neck, I will be praying, a lot, about this."

"That's the spirit."

"Well, we'd best be hanging up." She laughed out loud. "What an archaic expression! We don't actually hang up cell phones."

"No, but expressions do linger," Erin said, wondering if Melissa would begin expounding on other outmoded terms.

"I need to get to the store and pick up a few things. My dad is coming over for dinner tonight."

Her breath caught in the back of her throat. Erin managed to wish Melissa a happy evening, ended the call, and had a good cry. For the first several weeks after her father's death last spring, each day, Erin had a weeping session of varying duration. Then she started going a couple of days without tears and after the wedding, she made it through an entire dry-eyed week. At this point, a sudden sight, sound, or mention of something related to her dad, whether his favorite song on the radio or spotting cookies he loved at the grocery store would turn on the waterworks. Erin would never be able to have her dad over for dinner again. Deeply inhaling, she checked her watch. Ethan wouldn't be home for another hour and a half. Sure, she had laundry and packing to do, but something more pressing had just come up.

"Oh, my! What brings you here today, Erin?" Audrey's face glowed. Then she gave a small hop. "Wait a minute. Are we supposed to go shopping, and I forgot?"

Erin put the donut box and cardboard tray with two cups of takeout coffee on her mom's kitchen table then gave her a lingering hug.

"No, Mom, you didn't forget a thing. I just thought how nice a visit with you would be before I head off to Chicago."

You just never know how long you have with your parents.

She'd heard about the dazzling light people said they had seen during near-death experiences and briefly considered whether the intensity shone like this television studio's.

Erin had done a handful of radio shows and three book signings with Derek, but her inaugural TV appearance created a sensation around the crown of her head like gulping three cans of soda in rapid succession. She squinted until her pupils adjusted to the artificial brightness, then her gaze swept over the coolest, most put-together assortment of people she'd ever been with in one place. She fought back a giggle when a line from a seventies' song randomly popped into her head: "and his hair was perfect." Her emotions jackknifed. *Whatever made me wear this black suit? I look like a Philadelphia lawyer.* She briefly considered making a run for the door she and Derek had just come through, offering her apologies while feigning sudden illness. She closed her mouth and breathed in slowly through her nose, counted for several seconds, then slowly released the air through her mouth.

Derek wore a suit as well, but he managed to pull off his academic vibe in this Millennial-dominated setting. Maybe everyone expected a venerable author to look like he did, but if Erin were going to continue making public appearances, she was going to have to update her wardrobe. And make sure she packed an extra pair of pantyhose. The thought of the run at the top of her right thigh creeping into view on camera chilled her to the core. Deciding she could do nothing about her appearance now, Erin changed her attitude. Standing taller, she donned a cloak of learned sophistication, hoping she did a good job of faking it.

An unnaturally thin woman in black yoga pants and a white blouse strode toward her and Derek offering something Erin might have mistaken for a smile. "Dr. McCutcheon! How very nice to have you with us today!" She held out a skeletal hand. "I'm Mindy Conrad, producer of *A.M. Chicago*. We're just going to take you to makeup now if you'll follow me." She began walking down a hallway without waiting for his response, and Erin brought up the rear.

They landed in a large room with more blazing lights, and Mindy waved her hand toward a striking brunette standing by a salon-type table with a mirrored backdrop. "Dr. McCutcheon, this is Arnotta, who will be doing your makeup. Arnotta, take good care of him. This is America's professor you know."

America's professor? That's new.

Erin studied the makeup artist's arresting eyebrows and flawless teeth.

"Welcome, Dr. McCutcheon. It's an honor to meet you. My parents just love your books."

She winced at the obvious reference to his age, which Erin knew to be in the low seventies.

"I'm pleased to meet you as well," he said.

"Won't you just sit in this chair, and we'll get started?"

Derek didn't budge. "Of course, just as soon as you also take care of my associate." He turned toward Erin, whose ears had turned red.

"Oh, Dr. McCutcheon, I'm so sorry." Mindy went to Erin and gave her a full-on once over. "You can come to the green room while he gets made up. That's where you'll be watching the interview."

Erin's stomach clenched. Derek had schlepped her all the way to Chicago to appear with him on this show, and now this brusque little producer treated her like she was wearing last year's fashions, which she was.

The author stepped away from the makeup station and stood next to Erin. "My dear Ms. Conrad, had you shown my colleague the most basic common courtesy, you would have given me an opportunity to introduce you to Dr. Erin Miles Bassett, my coauthor. We will be appearing together on your show."

"I do beg your pardon, Dr. McCutcheon. Uh, hello, Dr. uh ..."

Erin found her voice, and her spirit, the kind she used in the classroom with upstart undergrads. "Bassett. Dr. Erin Miles Bassett." She took hold of the producer's hand and shook the limp appendage.

Mindy broke away, putting on her designer reading glasses and consulting a clipboard while the makeup artist twirled a brush, shifting from one foot to the other. "I only have here that you'll be on air."

"I assure you, Ms. Conrad, there was no mistaking the terms of my appearance when I spoke to Charlie Peevy."

"Did I hear someone mention my name?"

Mindy blanched.

Derek broke into a grin. "Charlie, my friend, I was hoping you'd be here today."

"Now how could I miss seeing my old college roommate?"

Erin watched them backslap each other like schoolboys.

"Charlie, this is Dr. Erin Miles Bassett, my talented coauthor. This will be her first on-air appearance with me."

The man turned his smile on Erin and, though not as luminous as Arnotta's, it was far more genuine. "Welcome, Dr. Miles. It's an honor to have you here with Derek today." He didn't seem to notice Erin's uncool outfit. "Mindy, make sure she gets one of our top people for makeup."

She went all sweetness and light. "Follow me, Dr. Bassett. I think you'll enjoy working with Andy."

She wanted nothing more than to settle into her first class seat, complements of Derek's publisher, and read her ancestor's journal on the way home—if she could stay awake. Not that she'd actually brought the little book with her. Paul had helped her scan the next few entries and printed them for her so she wouldn't be taking any risks of losing, or harming, the priceless volume. She looked over at Derek, more than twenty years her senior, and wondered how he could look as fresh as he had during their interview, like he'd downed a Red Bull.

Erin stretched her legs and took another look at the flight information board where she followed the progress of incoming and outgoing airlines, prepared to start boarding any time now. She gave a start when "Flight 63, ABE: 6:53 PM, On Time" suddenly switched to "Delayed. 7:20."

Derek was looking up at the posting too. "Isn't that your flight?"

"Yes."

"Fortunately the delay is only a half hour." He tilted his head, apparently used to such things.

"I see mine's still on time, 7:30." He'd be flying directly to Logan International, then getting a driver to take him to his Concord, New Hampshire, home just over an hour away.

She checked her watch: 6:10.

Derek set his *Smithsonian* magazine aside. "I felt so comfortable with you today on the show, iron sharpening iron, just like we do when we're writing together." He grinned. "I may just want you to come to all my TV and radio appearances."

A thrill ran through her, followed by a tensing in her shoulders. *This was fun, but I'm not sure I want to do this on a regular basis. It would mean too much time away from my family.* She was, however, constantly aware of the great privilege of being this icon's work partner. "You are very kind, Derek. We do seem to complement each other nicely."

He gave a laugh. "I'm reminded of a story I heard years ago about Fred Astaire and Ginger Rogers." He lowered his chin and looked at her over the top of his glasses. "You do remember them, don't you?"

"My mother used to watch their movies. They were a dream team."

"Dream team," he muttered. "Yes, they were. I recall some observer once said they fit together so well because Fred gave Ginger class, and she gave him sexiness."

She couldn't hold back a laugh.

He grinned. "I'm glad you didn't take it the wrong way. I often apply very general principles to specific contexts, and my wife tells me to be careful. I hope I didn't offend."

"Not at all."

By the time he rose to get on his plane a half hour later, Erin's flight had been pushed back yet again.

"Will you be all right?" Derek asked.

"Yes, I'm fine. Have a good trip home, and thank you again for insisting I appear with you today."

He turned out a puckish grin. "You didn't think I'd let that Mindy person have her way?"

He gripped and held her hand for a long moment. "Are you sure you're okay now?"

"Absolutely."

"Then bye for now, Ginger."

"All right, Fred."

She watched him disappear into the crowd moving toward their gate. Fifteen minutes later, her delayed flight turned into "canceled."

She texted Paul from the airport shuttle, rumbling through town to an airline-designated hotel. She would have called except the decibels in the crowded vehicle had risen to the level of a locust invasion. She was definitely not of the ilk who hollered personal information into a cell phone in public, and Erin would have had to holler really loudly here.

> There was engine trouble, so I'm grounded until tomorrow morning. My new direct flight leaves O'Hare at 6:14 a.m.. On my way to hotel with other refugees. Airline is footing the bill. Miss you! Will call from the hotel. XXOO

She raised her head and took in the choked lanes of traffic wondering how there could be so much congestion this many hours past the evening rush. A notification on her phone drew her away from the blaring headlights and atonal horns.

> Bummer. We were looking forward to picking you up at the airport. Be safe. I'm glad all went well with your interview at least! We watched the livestream and thought you did great. Love you back.

She'd been too exhausted to deal with one more social encounter today and had settled on the small luxury of a twenty-dollar burger from room service. Just after calling in her order, she rang up Paul, speaking to him and Ethan about her adventures, and hearing about her son's play practice plus a mysterious bill from the water company. Her eyes glowed as she considered the blessing of having a husband waiting for her, and someone to look after Ethan when she had to be away. Before hanging up, she said, "I'll be home tomorrow morning and will have plenty of time to rest up for that board meeting."

"I'll be there to pick you up," Paul said.

"Can't wait. Uh, how's it going with you and Ethan?"

"We're doing quite well."

"No missed buses or late bedtimes?"

"Well ..."

"What happened?

"I forgot to pack his lunch yesterday."

"That's not too bad. I've done the same thing."

She wondered how Ethan felt about having Paul in his everyday life, but gleaning such information from a tight-lipped middle schooler would have to wait.

"I love you."

"I love you back," she said.

Erin ended the call and sighed, filled with longing for her new husband and anxiety about the gathering in which her status with the Kichline Center would be determined. Although she'd always worked well with the other board members, Erin wondered how many of them would come to her aid now, and how many were beholden to Craig Reldan for any number of reasons. Before she got herself worked into a lather, she reached for the leather folder containing a few scanned pages of her grandfather Peter's journal. She wanted nothing more than to lose herself in his life. So many times in the past, knowing what he'd gone through had infused fresh courage and faith into her own circumstances, such as after Jim died. Erin had learned her ancestor had also lost his wife at a similar age. Who knew? Maybe there'd be something to glean from his story yet again.

She set the laptop across her knees and lifted the first page of the diary to begin entering the German words she didn't understand. Reading printed German in a text book was one thing; discerning the meaning of centuries-old handwriting was another animal entirely.

Painstakingly, she typed each word, one after another, with such intensity she didn't realize two hours had passed. Sometimes, she had no clue of the meaning and filled the spaces with parenthetical guesses. Her feet had fallen asleep, and she moaned while jiggling them to clear the pins and needles sensation. While she'd been translating, the meaning of individual words had stood on their own; she hadn't seen the forest for the trees. Now she was ready to look at the whole picture. After stretching as if she were warming up for a run, she went back to the bed and read the fruit of her labor.

> October 9, 1781
> Easton, Penna.
> Saw Rbt Traill today. We share a mutual desire for the war to come to an end, heartened by largely positive reports from the south.
> War is a wearisome thing, although at times, necessary. I am happy most people in the village and Northampton Cty have supported the Cause, although some have not. Like those Mennonites Andrew had dealings with in Bedminster. Even in one family there was division. My bro. Charles told me how Andrew brought the stubborn father food and firewood when illness felled the entire family. What will become of such as these when the war ends remains unknown, but we must find a way to turn former enemies to friends, to beat those swords into plowshares, that our experiment in liberty may flourish.

She wondered who that family was. Although she didn't know, Erin's spirit lifted at the mention of her Uncle Andrew's kind act toward someone who seemed against the American Cause, and Peter's desire for reconciliation. She continued reading.

October 11, 1781
Easton, Penna.
Pastor Rodenheimer gave me a most peculiar message today in form of a letter addressed to me but in care of the German Reformed Church. Written on good paper, sealed impressively, the letter was poorly written nonetheless. And not really a letter at all. More of a summons. I have been implored to a rendezvous in German Valley in two days. Catherine expressed concern. I am deeply curious.

Erin raised her eyes to the ceiling where the hotel room's smoke detector blinked red. The journal was reading like a Hercule Poirot novel, containing the intriguing mentions of unnamed Mennonites who had fallen from the community's good graces, and now, an enigmatic summons. Except this wasn't fiction. She happened to glance at the numbers on the bedside clock and gasped—nearly one o'clock. She briefly considered staying up since she only had a couple of hours to catch any sleep at all before meeting the airport shuttle, but brain fog overtook her, and she crawled into bed.

CHAPTER SIX

"I have a bad feeling about this, Peter."

He rested a hand on Catherine's forearm, forcing her to stop knitting as if her life depended on completing this sock before going to bed. "What kind of feeling?"

She pinched her lips together, looking toward the fire crackling in the parlor grate. "Perhaps someone is lying in wait for you to, to do you harm."

He stifled the harrumph rising to his lips. "A trap?"

"Y-yes, a trap."

He grappled to understand the fear that caused her to be so pale. Catherine had always been so stalwart in the face of danger, and this was hardly marching as to war or unpleasantries he'd confronted as sheriff. Why was she treating the strange summons with more trepidation?

He pulled the letter from his waistcoat and plucked reading glasses from the side table. "My dear wife, this is not the writing of a dangerous person."

"How do you know?"

For a moment, he thought his spouse looked exactly like seven-year-old Elizabeth right down to the quivering lower lip. He would present this as logically as possible. "You see, the stroke of the pen is light as a woman's and although badly written, the words are neat, almost florid. This appears to be the product of a distressed woman's hand and mind."

She shook her head. "I don't understand why this person had the letter delivered to the pastor and not to you."

He took a deep breath, his patience wearing thin. "My dear wife, I mentioned several times our new postal delivery man has been sending people the wrong mail. You took Robert Traill's to his home just last week."

"What are you going to do?"

"I am going to see what this is about."

His wife's eyes appeared overly bright. "Not alone?"

He certainly didn't relish the thought of being dragged away from home and family to encounter who-knew-what kind of problem, but he lived by the teaching of his mother, *to whom much is given, is much required.* He leaned back. "What do you suggest?"

"Take Peter or Andrew or Jacob."

"I would do so if they were not all busy with their work."

"Then take William or Joe."

He bit back a laugh. At roughly eleven years of age, Joe was hardly old enough to protect Peter. He wouldn't dignify her absurd suggestion about the boy with a response, but he would mention William. "Catherine, William has his hands quite full keeping up with furniture orders and lending a hand at the saw mill."

"Surely he can get away for a day or two to assist you." She pleaded like a child. "Please just ask."

Perhaps his brush with death as a prisoner of war had been a greater ordeal for her than he had understood. He gazed upon her earnest, lovely face, his heart filling with compassion. "If doing so will ease your mind, I will see him first thing in the morning. I intend to leave shortly afterwards. Tomorrow is the twelfth, and I'd like to arrive in German Valley with a day to spare."

She closed her eyes and nodded. "Thank you, Peter. You can ask him tonight."

Why was she pushing him? He'd acquiesced to her need, and now all he wanted to do was sit by the fire in peace, smoke his pipe, and read *The Pennsylvania Gazette*. "This will wait until tomorrow." He plucked a brass box of tobacco from the table to get his intentions across.

"You misunderstand, darling. William is here, in the house."

"Here?" He paused, his hand in midair.

"Yes, in the kitchen."

His eyes narrowed. "I didn't see him come in. What's he doing in the kitchen?"

Catherine gave him a look he'd seen a time or two before, which translated into English meant something like, "I cannot believe you don't understand what is patently obvious to everyone else."

He surrendered, with a proviso. "I will ask him as soon as I get in the reading I was intending to do when we retired here after dinner."

She opened her mouth, closed it just as quickly, and took up the sock.

"Mama! Mama!" Elizabeth's voice fluttered like a distress flag down the stairs.

Catherine bolted from her chair, dropping her knitting on the floor. "Yes, dearest, I'm coming." She looked over her shoulder. "She's probably had a nightmare."

Peter lowered his paper and watched his wife sail from the room with the small limp that had marked her gait since a wagon accident in her youth had taken her parents to eternity. After reading the same sentence multiple times without comprehension, he stood and flexed his tall body, feeling all fifty-eight of his years imposing themselves against his lower back. Perhaps Bett had some shoo fly pie left over from dinner. That and a cup of tea would hit the spot on a cold night. His southern housekeeper had learned to make one of the best pies in Easton, a conviction he shared with no one, lest he find himself on the receiving end of feminine Pennsylvania Dutch ire. While satisfying his sweet tooth, he could also find out if William was available.

Peter strode down the hall to the back of the house hearing a low-throated giggle. Entering the room with its fragrance of smoked meat, ashes, and cinnamon, he saw Joe with his head resting on his arms against the table, apparently asleep, and William leaning into Bett Reynolds's personal space, caressing a curl around his forefinger. The look on her face reminded him of his seven-year-old daughter, innocent yet flirtatious. In his moment of revelation, Peter chortled. He might be slow on the uptake, but even he recognized romance when it hit him in the face.

All at once Bett straightened. William jumped up so hastily his chair rocked backward, and he snatched it, preventing the chair—and himself—from tumbling over. Joe jerked his head up.

"C-c-colonel sir. Do you be needin' somethin'?" A flush crept across the woman's coffee-colored face.

"Why, yes, Bett. I am in search of a snack."

She hurried toward a sideboard and produced a redware pan containing two wedges of pie. Her hand trembled as she dug out the biggest slice. "What do you want to wash it down with?"

"Some tea if you please." He leaned against the door frame, amused by the situation.

She nodded and turned, hanging a copper kettle on a hook over the fire.

"William. Joe." He nodded at them in turn.

"Colonel." William gave a short bow.

"Hello, Colonel Sir Peter."

Peter mussed Joe's hair. "Shouldn't you be getting to bed, young man? This is a school night after all."

"Yes, sir, colonel." He popped up. "Goodnight, Bett. Goodnight, William." He grabbed a paper from the table bearing what appeared to be some type of German folk art.

"What is that you have there, son?" he asked.

Joe's face flushed. "Well, sir, I've been learning how to draw some of Mr. Spangenberg's *fraktur*."

"I would like to see that." Peter reached for the artwork and studied its careful lines and bursts of color, whimsical figures of farmers, birds, and flowers. "You did this?"

"Yes, sir, Mr. Kichline." Joe shifted from one foot to the other as he looked at William as if wondering what he should say or do.

"Joe seems to have a fine talent, Colonel."

"Yes, William, I would agree." He handed the paper back. "Very nice, Joe."

"Thank you. Goodnight. Goodnight, Bett and William." He hurried from the room.

While he waited for his tea, Peter took a seat at the table bearing the marks of three decades' worth of food preparation, commencing with his beloved first wife, Margaretta. He ran a finger along one of the deeper gashes. "Please have a seat, William. How is your work coming along?"

The young man let out a huge breath as he lowered his lean body into the chair he'd just vacated. "Just fine, sir."

Bett spoke up, her chest expanding. "He's making a cabinet for Mr. Levers, who's payin' him a fine wage."

"Is that so?" He leaned back, welcoming details.

"Yes, sir. I've been workin' on it day and night. He wants it by day after tomorrow, and I'm just about finished." His cheeks colored. "I just stopped in for a short visit, you see."

Peter saw. He also realized there would be no asking William to go with him to German Valley, not when Robert Levers had commissioned him on a deadline. Peter's chin lifted as he considered how far William had come since Peter had rescued him and Joe from the slave auction six years ago in Philadelphia. Now a free man, William had earned the respect and admiration of the village through his service to the Cause, as well as his fine carpentry skills. The pulpit he had fashioned for the new church had wowed Eastonians, who now clamored for his services.

"I would enjoy seeing the cabinet, William. I know you'll do a fine job."

"Thank you, sir. I will show you tomorrow if you'll stop by the sawmill."

"I will be going to New Jersey, but I'll come before I cross over."

Bett's eyelids opened wide. "I didn't know you were leaving, Colonel Kichline."

"The decision has just been made this evening."

"You will need provisions."

Peter could almost see her thoughts whirring into action, figuring what she had on hand and how she could provide for him, along with her questioning why he was leaving so suddenly and whether anything might be wrong.

"Will it just be you going, sir?"

"For now, yes, but possibly another." He said this despite not being sure about the "another" part.

"I'd best prepare for two then."

William clapped his big hands together. "Well, then, goodnight, sir." He turned to Bett and said with comic formality. "Goodnight, Miss Reynolds."

She looked down, her eyelashes fluttering. "G'night, Mr. Carpenter."

Peter was considering how much he liked the surname William had chosen when a sound at the front of the house caused their ears to perk up.

"Is that someone at the door?" Bett asked.

When people came around late into the night, Peter knew they usually didn't bear any kind of good tidings. He cast a longing look at the uneaten pie and, seeing steam rising from the kettle, excused himself. "If you would please prepare two cups of tea, Bett, instead of one."

She nodded her head and reached for a second cup and saucer.

William followed Peter down the hallway where the former opened the door, cocking his head to the side upon seeing the minister.

Pastor Rodenheimer apologized for the third time since entering the Kichline residence where he now sat in the parlor with Peter. William had greeted the cleric, then slipped into the night to return to his residence at the sawmill.

"I do hope I am not disturbing you."

He swallowed a large bite of pie before answering, wishing Rodenheimer would eat so Peter didn't feel quite so gluttonous. "You must put yourself at ease, Pastor. I was just getting a snack when you came and was, and am, very much awake."

"But your dear wife, and your household?"

He waved a hand. "What has brought you here? You appear preoccupied."

Rodenheimer's chest rose and fell, then he leaned closer. "I have not been able to clear my mind of the letter you received earlier today."

The sound of footsteps on the stairs diverted the men's attention to the figure of Catherine as she descended. "I thought I heard you talking to someone," she said, addressing her husband.

Rodenheimer and Peter both rose as she entered the room. "Good evening, Mrs. Kichline. I am so very sorry to have disturbed you."

"Not at all, Pastor. Our Elizabeth has just fallen asleep, and I am still very much awake." She raised and tilted her right hand to the side. "Please, do sit down." She sat on the couch opposite their chairs.

"Would you like some tea, my dear?" Peter knew there wasn't any more pie but his wife seldom ate after the evening meal.

"No, thank you. Please enjoy your desserts."

Rodenheimer spoke up. "I was just telling your husband I have not been able to put the letter he received today out of my mind. I-I ..." His voice trailed off as he picked at the fabric of his breeches. "Well, in my life, I have on several occasions had what I refer to as a kind of *Vorahnung*."

Catherine's face paled. "A premonition?"

"Well, yes." Rodenheimer leaned forward, resting his elbows on his knees. "I have learned to pay close attention to them since an incident a few years before I came to Easton."

Peter suddenly forgot about the pie.

"You see, I was on a journey and staying at a tavern when I awakened in the middle of the night with a compulsion to go downstairs. At first I ignored the impulse, but when it grew more persistent, I ventured to the first floor where I found a man lying so close to the fireplace, his coat was just about to catch the flames. I pulled him away, and he was spared a most terrible ordeal."

Catherine's hand flew to her throat. "Oh, pastor!"

Peter cocked his head. "Are you saying this current situation is similar?"

"Yes, Colonel Kichline, I believe so."

He sat at the edge of his chair, his left calf tingling, the atmosphere spiritually charged.

"In that particular instance, you were compelled to do something specific. What of now?"

"I am not exactly sure beyond a strong sense you must answer this unknown person's summons." He raised his hands, palms up.

"But couldn't he be in danger?" Catherine asked.

Rodenheimer pursed his lips. "I do not believe he will be, but we must still be circumspect."

Peter avoided, yet felt the weight of, Catherine's gaze. "I plan to leave tomorrow."

Rodenheimer sat up straighter. "Part of my coming here tonight was to offer my company. I can be of assistance as I know the pastor of the Lutheran congregation in German Valley. This may be of help to you since the writer of the letter asked you to meet there." He glanced at Catherine. "Perhaps my being with your husband will in part alleviate any fears you may have, Mrs. Kichline."

"Oh, Pastor Rodenheimer, that would be wonderful!" Her eyes glistened. "Your going would very much set my heart at ease."

Peter took a swig of hot tea, letting the tannic acid brace him. "I am grateful for your offer, Pastor, and I accept with deep gratitude." *I'm not sure, but at this moment I am sensing my own Vorahnung about going.*

CHAPTER SEVEN

Erin staggered from the hotel room, bumping her suitcase behind her, hoping, quite possibly against hope, she hadn't forgotten any personal belongings. In the lobby, she joined a wave of airport refugees gathered outside, hunkering into her coat to ward off pre-dawn Chicago's unyielding cold. Even at four-thirty, vehicles clogged the lanes. Mercifully, the shuttle pulled up minutes later and swung open its doors, and the travelers piled in. She dozed off on the trip to O'Hare, roused from slumber by a wide-awake grandma tapping Erin's knee with the tip of her cane. "Better wake up, sweetie. We're here."

"Huh? Oh, right. Thanks." She blinked to clear sleep from her eyes and rose, staggering when the van lurched to a full stop. Sheeplike, she followed the others to security, then to get her boarding pass, realizing she could have completed this step electronically. *Jim always took care of the details. I really need to learn how to navigate flying on my own, especially if I'm going to be doing this frequently.*

She brought up the rear of the line, leaning on the extended handle of her suitcase with a bulging tote bag on top. Out of the blue, a groan began in the near distance, gathered strength, and rumbled toward her. She tapped the shoulder of the man in front of her, a rather large fellow blocking her view of the counter. "Excuse me. What's happening?"

He growled across his right shoulder. "Our flight's been delayed."

"Delayed?"

"Delayed."

The word was a cold washcloth slap to the face. "But why?"

"Does it matter? I'm going to be late for a very important meeting. Again." He cursed loudly enough to register his anger with the airline employee handling check-ins.

Although she craved information, Erin knew this was not her man. She heard dribs and drabs of muttering and cussing until she came face to face with the vilified desk clerk. Standing straight, chin up, the woman with the swanky little scarf seemed perfectly composed. She did, after all, work at an airport notorious for delays and cancellations.

"Your last name please?"

"Bassett." Even in her consternation, Erin relished the sound of it on her lips.

"First name?"

"Erin. Erin Miles Bassett."

The impeccably made up eyes turned from her to the screen while she typed. "I see you're going to Lehigh Valley with this group."

"Yes."

"Unfortunately, that flight has been delayed by two hours."

"Do you know why?"

She gazed at Erin. "This flight originated in Denver, and they had heavy snows last night."

"Oh." She took some comfort in a weather-related problem, as opposed to engine trouble.

More tapping of the keys. "I can get you on the next flight to Lehigh Valley which leaves Chicago at ten-fifteen. Would you like me to book that for you?"

She had dragged herself out of bed for this. Collecting her irritation and expelling it through a deep breath, she asked, "When is arrival?"

"Two-ten this afternoon. For your inconvenience, I can put you in business class."

I'll still be able to make the meeting, although I was hoping to get more rest than this will allow me once I get home. Stupid meeting. Stupid Craig Reldan. Life was so perfect until he opened his big mouth, throwing his weight around like he always does. Well, I'm not going to let him ruin things.

"Excuse me, ma'am?"

Erin's lip curled. "I am already traveling first class."

"Oh, yes, of course. Shall I book this flight for you?"

"Yes, please do."

She finished the transaction and stuffed the boarding pass in her purse, figuring she might as well go to the now-familiar lounge and get some coffee. Putting a shine on the tarnished experience, she told herself she'd have enough time to buy souvenirs for Ethan, Paul, and her mom. Erin had decided whenever she traveled without them she would buy a local candy or confection for her son, a history-themed book for Paul, and a spoon for Audrey's collection. She could refresh her stash of magazines or buy a new book for herself, or better yet, translate the rest of the excerpt she'd brought of her ancestor's journal. Maybe the delay wouldn't be so bad after all.

"So, these are the candies Chicago is famous for?"

"They certainly are." The clerk, an octogenarian if he was a day, provided relief from the robotic millennial who'd taken Erin's coffee and breakfast order. The only sign of life had emerged when Erin requested salsa instead of cream cheese for her blueberry bagel. Wearing a Cubs hat nearly as old as himself, this guy was chatty. She needed chatty.

He picked up a box from the counter behind him opening it to reveal compartments of confections. "You got your Wrigleys gums and your Lemonheads, your Tootsie Rolls and Snickers, your Brachs and your M & M's and, of course, you can't forget your Cracker Jacks."

"I never realized these candies originated here." Her heart warmed at the sight of jelly nougats, her Grammy Ott's all-time favorites.

"They most certainly do." His small chest expanded to its full extent. "Can I wrap up a box for you?"

"Better make it two." They'd fit easily in her tote bag, and she thought her mom would enjoy some.

"Where are you headed?"

"Allentown, Pennsylvania."

"Nice place. I was there years ago visiting an aunt on my mom's side. Isn't there an amusement park there?"

"Yes. Dorney Park."

"That's the place." He finished wrapping the packages and rang up the sale.

Since he was so congenial, Erin figured he wouldn't mind dispensing some advice. "I'm looking for a bookstore and don't want to get lost in this maze." She stretched out her right arm to indicate O'Hare's formidable vastness.

"You bet. First time I came here, I got so lost I ended up on the L going downtown."

She narrowed her eyes, wondering if he was trying to pull the wool over them.

"So, then, see that coffee shop down at the end of this hallway?" She nodded. "When you get there, hang a right. You'll see a watch store on the left. Just after that go left, and you'll see your bookstore."

Erin repeated the instructions and accepting the packages of candy, she thanked him and moved with the crowd toward her next stop.

She took all of five minutes selecting a pictorial volume about the Chicago Fire for Paul, grinning as she remembered the first coffee table book they purchased—in Europe at the Heidelberg University store, a volume about the city's origins and history. There in the place her ancestor had been educated, they decided whenever they traveled, they would bring back a photographic history to remind them of their journeys. The thought of her honeymoon sweetened her, golden days traipsing around ancestral villages in Germany, Switzerland, France, and England, walking in the footsteps of their forebears as she and Paul came together to fashion a new family.

She couldn't wait to be back in her husband's arms, but for now, she hustled to the lounge to read more of her grandfather Peter's journal. Erin settled into the leather chair with her laptop, her little portfolio, and a paper cup of tea. Thirty minutes later, she had translated another segment.

> October 12, 1781
> Easton, Penna.
> Re. the strange letter that came to me. I believe someone to be in trouble, and told Catherine my Christian duty is to provide aid if possible. Wm was unavailable to accompany me, but Pastor Rodenheimer came by late at night volunteering his services. He said he couldn't get the thought out of his mind, and might be particularly helpful since he is acquainted with the pastor in German Valley. There I am to meet the writer of the letter. We set out tomorrow.

Erin frowned. *I wonder if "Wm." might be "William" and if so, who was he?* She couldn't recall any past relatives bearing the name. *Maybe he was a friend, or he worked for Grandfather Peter. Or he could have been a soldier hanging around Easton, but why would he be available to Peter? Wouldn't he have his own duties?'* Then she remembered. *He was at that time Lieutenant of Northampton County, so he was still in an official military capacity.* For a moment, the airport receded, and she found herself dwelling in his eighteenth century home, picturing a low-beamed roof, well-made furniture, and a cheering fire.

"Excuse me."

She came to attention and removed her reading glasses, seeing the airline's well-groomed representative standing before her. "Oh, hello." Time traveling, even mentally, took some flexibility.

"Dr. Bassett?"

"Yes."

"I'm afraid I have some bad news."

Erin flinched. "What's wrong?"

"Your flight has been canceled."

She gaped at the woman. "Canceled? But it was just delayed."

"Yes, bad luck I know. If you come with me, we'll get you on a different one."

This was just. Too. Much.

When the notification sound pinged, Erin checked her text messages. *Good morning! Hopefully you're on a plane and heading back to your family by now.*

"No, Derek," she muttered, "I'm not on a plane heading back to my family. I'm stuck at O'Hare. Again." She tapped, *Good morning to you as well. There was yet another cancellation, and I won't be getting home until this evening.*

She waited for his response, staring at the screen.

That's just awful! So very sorry to hear this.

She wished he'd said more, but then, what more could he say?

Speaking with Paul, she blundered her way through an explanation of the convoluted means of getting back to Lehigh Valley International, squinting at the scrawled notes in her travel journal.

"Okay, so, uh all flights are backlogging because of the, uh, earlier engine trouble, then the weather delays. They can reroute me through, well, some Florida airports, I forget which ones, I can't read my writing, or send me directly to Philadelphia so I'd arrive at six this evening, or I can wait for the next direct flight to Allentown, which would get me home around eight-thirty." She caught her breath, her sweaty palms blurring the ink.

"When would you get to Allentown if you take those connecting flights?" Paul asked.

"Uh, let's see here, ah ... right, if I go through Orlando, I'll get home at seven, and Ft. Lauderdale involves two layovers, and I'd be there by six-thirty." Erin clawed through her overly-full thoughts, reaching for clarity, coming up with heartburn.

Her husband spoke calmly, bringing the matter into sharper focus. "I just can't see you spending over a dozen hours in multiple airports where there could always be more delays for whatever reason.

Maybe you're just not meant to be at the meeting tonight, Erin."

She sucked in a deep breath, on the verge of bursting into tears. "Not be there? How can I not be there? Craig would get exactly what he wants then." She started imitating him. "'See what I mean, people? Not only is she not overseeing the renovation, she's so preoccupied with other projects she can't even make this meeting.'"

Paul chortled. "You sounded exactly like him." When she didn't answer, he continued. "I'll go. I'll represent you. After all, I am acting in an advisory capacity to the Kichline Center, I am your husband. I have this Erin. Try not to worry."

She drew his soothing words to herself, allowing them to enfold her in their comforting embrace. Paul was an attorney, level-headed, fair. He would know how to make a solid case for her. Jim had always had her back as well. She remembered the time she'd bought her first new car, which turned out to be a lemon. She kept bruising her shins kicking the walls of the dealership to get satisfaction, until Jim stormed the gates. She had a new car within twenty-four hours. The realization of being blessed to have had two such husbands strengthened her in this exasperating moment. A further startling thought pounced and grabbed hold. *Even if the board decides not to keep me as director, I will still have the most wonderful life. As much as I want to run the Center, I already have so much.* She recalled a statement years before by a presidential candidate who told an interviewer even if he lost, he would be okay, he didn't need the highest office to be happy.

"Okay, Paul, I'm going to take the flight that gets me home by eight-thirty. And thank you. Thank you so much."

"I think that's the wisest choice, and I'll be there to pick you up, no matter what's happening at the meeting."

"Is Ethan doing okay with all these changes to my schedule?"

"He's fine, taking them in stride. He's a good kid."

Her heart warming, an unexpected thought alarmed her. "He can't stay home alone yet."

Paul gave a matter-of-fact response. "Oh, right. I'll just get Audrey to stay with him."

"Okay, but please don't tell her what's going on at the Center. You know how she gets."

"I'll tell her I'm covering for you at a meeting because your flight's been delayed." He paused. "I'm just so sorry you need to hang around that crummy airport all day. What will you do with yourself?"

She hadn't thought about that. "Oh, I don't know. Read. Translate the diary. Walk. Eat. Sleep. I hardly slept last night. Fortunately, this first-class lounge is quite comfortable, and decently removed from all the noise and clamor." She had an inspiration. "Could you possibly scan more pages of the diary and email them to me? I'm nearly finished with the few I have."

"Sure. I know what I did before, and I'll be happy to send more." A long moment later, he spoke again. "I've been thinking about something, wondering if I should even bring this up, but the thought persists."

Her heart pounded. "What?"

"Well, in the end, do you really want the Kichline Center position, Erin?"

She was at first too startled to comment.

"I know Craig is wrong about your not overseeing the renovation, and I know you'd make a strong ED, but at the heart of it all, do you want to direct the Center? I really hesitated to say something, Erin because I'll support you no matter what, but consider how you do so much– writing books and traveling, taking care of your mother and raising a middle schooler, DAR ..."

Erin realized he hadn't mentioned "having a new husband," but building a marriage took as much effort as any of these other aspects of her life. Were his words a kind of confirmation? Quite unexpectedly peace began smoothing her ruffled mood.

"Craig is an unjust man who has hurt you, but as I look past my own resentment toward him, I can't seem to avoid this other question. I don't know if God put this on my heart, but I couldn't seem to shake this. The last thing I want is to hurt you. I wouldn't blame you for being angry with me. Anything that's best for you is what I'll get behind. That's where I'll always be."

She released the breath she'd been holding. "Quite frankly, I've been having similar thoughts."

"The two become one."

After they ended the call, she shuffled back to the airline agent and settled her itinerary.

"If you like, I can arrange for you to do some sightseeing while you wait," the woman said.

Erin pursed her lips. "Thank you, but I'll be fine here."

She claimed a comfortable leather chair and, leaving her bag, wandered to the food bar for a muffin and coffee with tabasco sauce. While she waited for the machine to run its cycle, she considered how her mother might have told her, "You're always wearing yourself to a nub, Erin. You need to choose what's most important and focus on that." Of course, Audrey would expect to be high on her daughter's list of priorities. Jim had also been quick to offer suggestions, almost parental. Paul wasn't. He provided insights when she asked, helped her work matters out for herself, then supported her decisions. That he'd even raised the question about her directing the Center wasn't like him, which made her wonder if the idea, and her own, hadn't come from higher up. She sucked in her breath. *What do you want me to do, Lord? Might this be your way of taking my work in a different direction?*

She had enough time on her hands to wait—and listen—for an answer.

CHAPTER EIGHT

The smell of cut wood, the sound of saws biting into lumber, and the sight of swirling dust particles seemed to salute Peter as he stepped inside his mill. His son, Jacob, looked up from his work and grinned upon seeing his father. He scattered debris from his leather apron and came forward, hand outstretched.

"Good morning, Father. How are you today?"

Peter gripped his dark-haired son's hand, heartened by his strong grip and ruddy mien. Although they had just been together the day before at supper, seeing his twenty-year-old offspring here instead of the gristmill cast him in a different, more independent, light. He knew the satisfaction of being able to count on Jacob and Andrew to run both businesses after proving their mettle during their father's imprisonment.

"I am quite well, thank you. I see you're helping your brother over here today."

Leaning against a nail keg, he said, "Andrew had to go to Bethlehem on some business, and I offered to help him. Bett told me you were going away today, but she didn't seem to know any more than that."

They exchanged a conspiratorial look. "I find her lack of insight most unusual." Peter's eyes gleamed. "She seems to know more about what is happening than I do on most days."

Jacob gave a laugh, then wiped a rogue wood chip from his right brow. "So, where are you heading?" He craned his neck as if looking for a horse or carriage.

"To German Valley with Pastor Rodenheimer on some personal business."

"I did hear something about an odd letter you received."

"Did Catherine tell you?"

He nodded his head. "I think she was hoping I could go with you, and I would have, except you know how busy the mill is just now."

"You were right to stay put, and I have the minister for a companion. I had a few minutes to spare, unencumbered, since Joe took my valise and a hamper of food to the manse for me."

"So, what was the letter about?" He narrowed his grey-blue eyes.

"The best I can discern from the brief summons is someone needs my particular help working out a problem."

"Then you're not worried?"

"Not in the least."

"Neither am I, Father." He gave a short laugh. "You can handle anything coming down any pike."

He smiled. "Thank you, Son."

Jacob straightened. "William told me to expect you, that you hoped to see his cabinet."

His son seemed as full of information as the town crier. "Did he finish the project?"

"He was up all night perfecting the piece, and he quite outdid himself." He lifted his thumb. "He's around the back in his shop."

"Then I'll go take a look. Good day, Jacob."

"Good day, Father. I, uh, will say a prayer for you."

Their eyes met, Peter buoyed by this show of faith in a son who displayed little interest in the church despite regular attendance. Once services ended, Jacob seemed to cast off its influence.

"Thank you." His voice sounded husky in his ears.

He went back outside into the flaming landscape, leaves crunching underfoot, listening to the orchestral Bushkill Creek, inhaling fall's smoky pungency. A squirrel dashed across his path, its cheeks heavy with acorns. Several feet ahead, he took in William Carpenter's tall figure presiding over a gleaming cabinet as if it were a small child being prepared by his mother for an Easter service. Its maker looked up and smiled at Peter as he drew closer to the outbuilding.

"Good morning, Colonel Kichline. How are you?"

"I am well, as you appear to be."

Despite his lack of sleep, William appeared fresh and eager. "I am just finishing the cabinet for Colonel Levers."

Peter willed himself not to mar the gleaming finish with a touch of his hand, although he would have enjoyed the silky feel of the cherry wood. When he stuck his hand in a pocket, Peter saw William let out a deep breath, probably of relief.

"I have seen no finer furniture in Philadelphia. This could stand side-by-side with the best of their cabinet makers."

The carpenter's chest expanded. "Thank you kindly."

"Should Colonel Levers change his mind, though I sincerely doubt he will, I would gladly feature this in my home." An idea burst upon him. "Perhaps, when you have the time of course, you could make one of these for Mrs. Kichline."

"I will be only too happy to, that is, if you don't mind waiting for me to finish another project." He looked up through the trees into the cloud-puffed sky. "I might be able to deliver one to you by Christmas."

Peter clapped his hands together. "What a splendid gift the cabinet will make, should you be able to complete it by then." He paused. "When will you bring this to Mr. Levers?"

"I'm ready now, Colonel. I have a cart to transport it."

"Would you like me to accompany you? I'm on my way to the church to meet Pastor Rodenheimer."

"Oh, that I would, sir. If you don't mind keepin' an eye on the cabinet so's it doesn't rattle around, I will pull the cart."

Peter realized the arrangement would better suit the craftsman if he guarded the furniture and Peter pulled the conveyance, but William would never ask such a favor. "I'll help in any way I can."

The two men set about swathing the fine piece in layers of plain-weave cotton bound with lengths of rope, then Peter helped William lift the cabinet onto the cart, insisting there was no need to call Jacob or one of the other men to assist. Despite upper left arm pain which Peter carried as a battle souvenir, he enjoyed this opportunity to bring his manhood to bear on the task.

Normally a soldier or a servant answered the door of Robert Levers's home on Northampton Street, but this morning, the man of the house stood before them, expectant. His eyes widened at the sight of Peter, and he clapped. "My good man! Not only do I receive my new cabinet, but I have opportunity to see my dear friend as well." He reached out and grasped Peter's hand. "And a very good day to you as well, William. I have been anticipating this moment all the night." He waved Peter inside, then called into the parlor, "Corporal Clayton, I have need of your help."

A muscular soldier appeared at once, a member of Levers's military retinue serving Northampton County's busiest leader. "Yes, sir?"

"Help William carry my new cabinet into the parlor, and be very careful."

"Yes, sir." Clayton went outside where William instructed him on how to handle the transfer.

Within a handful of minutes, the new cabinet outshone the very best of Mary and Robert Levers's array of fine furniture. Levers stood with his hands behind his back, running his eyes over his purchase with gleaming eyes and a high chin. "Beautiful," he muttered. "Just beautiful." When his wife entered the room, grayer-haired but more relaxed than the last time Peter had been here, she couldn't seem to take her eyes off the piece. Levers rested a hand on her broad shoulder. "Do you like it my dear?"

"More than I ever imagined. Thank you." She turned to William. "You are a fine craftsman. Thank you so much."

William bowed his head in acknowledgment of the praise. "I am glad you're pleased, ma'am."

She nudged her husband out of his reverie. "Yes, yes of course." He strode across the room to a writing desk the same color as the cabinet, and produced a leather wallet from which he removed several bills, which he handed to William. "I put in a little extra."

"Thank you, Colonel Levers."

"I couldn't be more pleased, William."

The cabinet maker shifted from one foot to the other. "If you'll excuse me, sirs, I need to get back to work."

"Yes, of course, William. Thank you again." Levers turned to Peter. "Do you have time for a coffee before you go about the rest of your business?"

He glanced at the mantel clock and realized he didn't need to be at the parsonage for at least a half hour. If he arrived early, he might be putting undo pressure on the minister and his preparations. "Yes, Colonel Levers, I believe I do."

Over the years, Peter had learned Robert Levers treated discourse like a Beethoven symphony, starting mellow, ending with a jolt. They engaged in pleasant chit chat for the first several minutes, then Peter readied himself for the shift he sensed was about to take place.

"My good man, I know you've had your hands quite full with your responsibilities as Lieutenant of the County, but I must ask if you might be able to supply me with a list for my own records of those who have refused to surrender arms or supplies."

This was a path Peter had not seen looming ahead, but he recovered his initial annoyance with no more than raised eyebrows. "Are you referring to the present or the past? I believe this subject has already been addressed."

Levers waved a hand bearing a pipe. "Past, present, it's all the same to me. Those who have not supported the Cause must be brought to justice."

Peter's expression tightened. "Aside from the Moravians and a few Mennonites in the county, we have had little difficulty with other residents. As you know, the German Lutheran and Reformed communities have fully supported the war, often to the point of personal deprivation."

"Yes, yes, this is true enough." Levers appeared to be biting the pipe's stem.

"Even many Moravians have provided succor for our wounded." He took a deep breath to steady his anger toward a man who had not infrequently been dismissive toward Northampton county's German population. In no way would he comply with a request smacking of the tyrannical leaders his family had fled in Europe. He didn't resist asking,

"Have you had any trouble with the Scottish or English demographic?"

Levers snorted. "The few who sided with the king have mostly pushed further west."

"Then the only names you need would be of farmers who resisted giving more than they could to keep their own families warm and fed, or peace Germans who were following the dictates of their own consciences. We have already required more than enough of them. There will be no punishment as far as I'm concerned." Peter crossed his arms over his chest.

Levers met his old friend's gaze, and broke into a nervous smile. "Steady, Kichline." He went quiet for a long moment. "I suppose you're right. At times, I can get a little carried away."

At times? Peter held his tongue, keeping his assessment to himself. Besides, he'd never heard Robert Levers admit he might be wrong about anything until that moment. The show of humility was a wonder to behold.

"I will tell you, while most of the Tories in the area have left, there was a bit of recent trouble from across the river."

Peter tipped his head to the side. "How exactly?"

"A couple of Lewis Gordon's sons live in the Jerseys, and they hold a grudge."

He pursed his lips, nodding. Easton's first attorney, Gordon had been an upstanding member of the village, widely respected, a leader of the Patriots, at least initially. Following repeated defeats of General Washington's army in the early months of the war, Gordon's convictions had gone wobbly. He'd resigned from the Committee of Safety and refused to take the Oath of Allegiance, so Levers had ordered he be put under house arrest. The business had left him embittered and broken in health, but shortly before Lewis's death, he had signed the Oath, and died mostly at peace.

"What did they do?" Peter asked.

Levers lowered his voice, inclining his head toward the hallway. "I don't want Mary to know. They sent me a threatening letter."

"Are you sure Lewis's sons sent it?"

"Although they didn't sign the letter, they made reference to my treatment of their father, so I assume they are the writers."

Peter knew Levers had ruffled any number of feathers in the county, but if the letter came from New Jersey and made reference to the Levers-Lewis affair, there was a good chance Levers had reached the correct conclusion.

"At any rate, I'm not afraid of them. I have a sentinel with me at all times." He muttered under his breath, "Blasted Tories."

Peter withdrew into his own thoughts, wondering whether the strange letter he'd received, also from New Jersey, might have anything to do with this matter. *Then again, Lewis's sons would not have written in such a poor fashion. On the other hand, if they're setting a trap, what better way to throw me off guard?* Maybe Catherine had been right.

CHAPTER NINE

"May I take that away for you?"

Erin looked up to see an airline lounge employee smiling, then inclining her head toward the detritus on the table.

"Ah, yes, thank you." She plucked herself out of her dreamworld and back to O'Hare Airport.

"Would you like a refill on your coffee?"

"Oh, uh, sure. Thanks." She decided against requesting tabasco sauce.

The sixty-something woman pointed to the computer screen. "That's some pretty old handwriting."

Erin bit back a sarcastic remark about prying into other people's business. *Am I tightly wound today, or what? I know these travel delays and tonight's meeting have me on edge, but this woman shouldn't bear the brunt of my frustration.* "Yes," she said, "this text is from the eighteenth century." Paul had graciously scanned and sent more diary pages.

"Oh my! You must be a professor."

Why did some people know how to push other people's buttons? Erin had been a professor, but what was she now, and what was she going to be? "Well, uh, I'm a historian, and I'm translating my ancestor's journal."

The woman's beginning-to-wrinkle face broke into a smile. "Imagine that! My family came here over a hundred years ago." She stood straighter. "You know, I always say people who lived way back then knew a lot more about life than we do today. Somehow all these devices we have haven't made us any smarter." Before Erin could respond, the hostess whisked away the dirty plate and cup and went, apparently, to secure a fresh cup of coffee. Erin's cell phone dinged, and she checked her texts to find a new one from Melissa. *Praying about tonight. It'll be okay. Promise. XO* She looked up to the ceiling, stretching her neck, realizing Melissa didn't know about the latest travel interruption. She decided to answer, *Thanks! Still in Chicago. Paul will represent me at the meeting tonight. Prayers are definitely needed.*

She turned her gaze toward one of the panoramic windows, watching clouds jousting against one another, considering what the hostess had just said, words finding their mark. What had her grandfather Peter written about Robert Levers? She returned her attention to her laptop and the part of the entry she'd just translated:

> Levers put an idea in my mind, and it clings to me like a burr. Lewis Gordon's sons have made threats against him because of what they perceived to be harsh treatment in the early days of the war. While this may be understandable— Levers did tend to overreach—might they also

harbor ill feelings toward me? Perhaps they do not realize I had by then resigned from the Committee to oversee the First Battalion. As I look toward the future, my hope and prayer are that Providence will grant our Cause ultimate success, and Loyalists will be assimilated back into the community. Although Robert might prefer to punish them, I think many have already been, and further penalties should be reserved only for the recalcitrant.

Erin leaned back into her seat and stared up at the ceiling for a long moment.

"Here you go." The hospitality hostess had returned with a fresh cup of hot coffee, its distinctly bitter aroma, a pleasant distraction.

"Thank you very much."

"Good luck with that journal, and let me know if you need anything else. I'm here all day."

And so am I.

She took a sip, flinching at the intense heat singing the tip of her tongue. Erin put the offending mug on the table to cool. *Just how concerned was Grandfather Peter about the letter being a Loyalist trap? No doubt he was 'packing,' as a former sheriff and military commander. I can't wait to find out who wrote that strange letter and for what reason.*

Something beside the mysterious nature of the letter and her ancestor's comments intrigued her—how he didn't seem in the least bitter toward Northampton County's Tories. She wondered how many of them there'd been, guessing not a lot since the bulk of the population was German, and those who supported the war outnumbered the pacifist Mennonites and Moravians. She'd once read a story about her grandfather Peter's actions toward the Bethlehem Moravians at the beginning of the conflict, how he'd gone there to confiscate their weapons for use by the nascent military. He hadn't taken them all, however, leaving enough behind for them to defend themselves. Then, right on his heels, George Taylor had gone over there and scooped up the weapons Peter had allowed them.

A man widely admired, known for fairness and compassion, Peter had nevertheless had a detractor, a soldier bearing the unfortunate surname "Musch." Back in 1776 he'd gone around town accusing the colonel of slowing the march to independence in the Pennsylvania Assembly in exchange for a bribe of land. Peter had fought doggedly to clear his good name of the false charge, while Musch ignored the Committee of Safety's repeated requests to substantiate the incrimination. Musch had refused until, after finally addressing the county's leaders, he stubbornly rebuffed their demand to recant after being found clearly in the wrong. They ended up declaring Musch dangerous and refractory, a public menace.

Erin tucked a leg underneath her and leaned back. *How did Grandfather Peter feel about Musch, especially since they lived in the same village and no doubt bumped into each other? I also wonder if the guy had any supporters, although I've never heard there were.* Her thoughts turned to Craig Reldan, her personal Musch, and Connie Pierce, who'd sworn she had nothing to do with Craig's scheme to remove Erin from the directorship. While Erin believed her, she wondered why Connie hadn't reached out since their awkward encounter at her house. Erin's chest ached at the thought of possibly losing both her job and a close friendship. She reached for a tissue in her tote bag and wiped her eyes, hoping no one was watching her private moment.

Her thoughts chugged down another track. *What's it going to be like to see Craig after all he's done and said against me? What if I feel like punching him in that nose he uses to look down at nearly everyone else? What if Paul confronts him at tonight's meeting? Although Paul doesn't have much respect for Craig, they do get along. And if Craig puts Paul on his enemies list, Paul could end up losing business just as he's building up his law practice.* She remembered how proud she'd felt when he got a commission as a legal consultant for Moravian College's development office. She fisted her hands, ready for a fight, until additional worries gnawed at her. *If the college doesn't employ me to be the director of the Kichline Center, we'll lose Ethan's tuition benefit, and since Paul doesn't have a regular income just yet, we may not have enough money to pay bills, let alone the mortgage. I suppose I could sell my house in Lansdale, and Paul has some savings, but then there's health insurance ...*

Erin sucked in her shallow breath, her heart beating arrhythmically. She grabbed the container of coffee, took a sip, then slammed the mug onto the table. *Blast that Craig Reldan! Why did he have to come barging into the perfect world I've created?*

She gasped so suddenly she didn't realize she'd done so until her immediate neighbor jerked his head in her direction. Her face colored, and she slumped into the chair, the lounge's sounds and smells receding. *The world I created? My perfect world? Since when have I been God?*

As if in answer, an unspoken voice impressed upon her, *For far too long.*

If she weren't in the midst of a dozen or so men and women in corporate and business casual attire, their heads bent over laptops or fingers nimbly working cellphones, Erin would have let out a loud "Ooof," one of her son's favorite expressions. This was an insight of biblical proportions, God's truth piercing her soul.

When had she first started erecting a perfect world for herself? She thought back to graduation from Lafayette when she'd left her hometown and family in pursuit of greener pastures. During her Villanova graduate studies, she'd met, then married Jim. Living an hour away from where she'd grown up, Erin was able to build an adult life on a firm foundation, apart from the family ruins. By keeping their drama at arm's length, Erin orchestrated and controlled her environment to eliminate as much unpleasantness as possible. She was the captain of her own fate, sailing on mostly calm waters, until Jim's unforeseen death had dashed her upon the rocks, until she began clinging to the Rock of her salvation.

Returning to Easton, she'd busied herself with recreating the world of her present and past family, striving to defend it against all enemies. No one was going to hurt her or her son. And she'd done a decent job, buying the home she'd loved as a child, teaching at Lafayette, helping her son know his family even as she came to better understand them as a mature adult who could hold her own now. She'd made new friends and, best of all, married Paul. Then, like a bratty seven-year-old, Craig Reldan had come along and kicked her tower of blocks.

She awakened to another truth and reached for her journal, scribbling, "tower of blocks." *God is the only strong tower I can run to, the only truly safe place to live, not in some pre-fabricated, so-called "perfect" world of my feeble design.*

Erin leaned back in the chair, her teeth sinking into the smooth surface of the pencil she gripped between her teeth. Her appointment to direct the Kichline Center for Colonial Easton History was a crowning moment of her carefully orchestrated life. How could she not be thrilled with work honoring her much-loved grandfather Peter, and grandmother Margaretta, and other people's families who had created a village in a virgin forest?

A thought sparked, and she quickly wrote in her own journal to capture the words before they might flicker away. *Grandmother Margaretta. Funny, I always feel so close to Peter, but his first wife is also my blood family. What was her life like in colonial Easton? She didn't live to see the Revolution, and neither did Anna Doll, his second, but Catherine did. She and my many times aunts and cousins were exactly the kind of unsung women of the Revolution Derek has me writing about. There is more than one way to honor my family's contribution to Easton's and America's history should the Center fall under Connie's direction.*

She suppressed another gasp. *I don't need this job. I want to be the director, but I don't have to be.* Erin closed her eyes for emotional privacy in this public place—and to pray. *I need to be about the work you give me, Lord, however you choose to give it to me whether I think it's perfect or not. The same with Paul. In standing up for what's right tonight, he will be doing your will.* She took a deep inhale. *So have your way tonight. Lead me, lead us, to your assignments. I'm sorry for trying to build a life as if I'm my own god. I've been wrong, and I need your help to follow you.*

She settled into the passenger seat after sharing warm kisses and hugs with her husband, seeing under the streetlights he wore the expression of a man who'd lost an altercation with a food processor. Her heart sank, even as faith rose to dispel the sudden tension in her temples. How the meeting had gone was the elephant resting between them on the console, allowing no room for small talk. She didn't ask for details until he'd worked his way through the arrivals area and pulled up to the traffic signal leading to Airport Road, choosing instead to text Ethan to say she had arrived safely and would be home soon. Then she blurted, "Well, how did it go?"

A dam broke, sweeping along the elephant.

Paul breathed out and, pulling onto the main road, said, "One meeting like that is enough for anyone's lifetime."

She wanted to get to the end of the book before starting the first chapter, but the story had to be told. "That bad?"

He nodded his head. "Where to begin?"

"Was anyone upset I wasn't there?"

"Surprised, but not upset. I explained, and they understood."

"I'll bet Craig was overjoyed."

Paul sniffed. "Bingo."

"And they let you speak for me?'

"They did."

"So, did I have mostly friends or detractors on the board?"

"At first, I'd say the board mainly wanted information. Reldan had spoken to each of them privately, so they already knew his thoughts about the matter, but once everyone was together, there seemed to be a higher plane."

"How do you mean?"

Paul turned left onto Route 22 East and merged into the light traffic. "It's like they were trying to give Craig an opportunity, in front of everyone, to lay out his case."

"How was he?"

"Smooth. I hate to say it, but he was pretty convincing, mainly stating how you weren't overseeing the reconstruction because you lacked expertise, that you weren't even teaching at the college, and how your writing projects kept you away most of the time."

"But they don't!"

He laid a hand on hers. "I explained you weren't going to be traveling all that much after the book launch."

Erin opened her mouth, then abruptly closed it. Paul seemed to think there was this initial spurt of running around, then not so much, the way she also had thought working with Derek would be like. Now she realized she didn't know what he expected, and she needed to discuss the matter with the renowned author in the near future to make sure they were on the same page. Fear showed up again, knocking loudly. *What if Derek says he can't work with me if I won't travel more than once a month, or whatever he has in mind?* To slow the march of anxiety, she breathed deeply and counted to seven, then slowly exhaled. *One problem at a time. I shouldn't be borrowing trouble. Besides, I don't have to make this or anything about my life or work perfect. God has this. He's in control here.*

"But wait, there's more."

Erin's eyes widened. "What else did he do, or say?"

"Craig said you were just a newcomer to Easton, and he strongly insinuated he could do a whole lot more financially for the Center if the board voted for Connie."

She laughed out loud. "I can't believe him! What really bothers me most, though, is how he has Connie under his thumb."

Paul waved a finger. "I think you'll be pleased to know Connie resigned her position in protest."

"C-connie resigned?"

"Indeed she did. She got up and said if you weren't directing the Center, she wanted no part of it."

She stood up for me! She truly is my friend. "What happened after that?"

"Well, the board went to pieces at that point. It was an hour and a half before a vote was taken, after several motions. Connie said she would run the Center only if you were appointed as president of the board. Craig was apoplectic. Then he convinced a majority to vote in favor of a resolution in which he would remain as president of the board, and Connie would run the Center along with you. She would be more administrative and full time, and you would be in charge of programming, a half-time position."

"But ..."

"The board voted in favor of your maintaining the benefits you currently have."

"Wow." Further words jostled for position in her mouth, but she couldn't quite decide which to speak first.

"I think the other board members were trying to be fair to you, Erin, especially when Craig started denigrating your qualifications. A number stood up for you, especially Herman Weinreich. Can you imagine how personally he was taking this attack against you?"

She closed her eyes, nodding her head.

"I think everyone understood Craig was upset over not being in the know when Lafayette's president and Herman first created the Center and appointed you. You know how Craig likes to run as much of Easton's show as possible."

"I know."

He cleared his throat. "I'm feeling hoarse. Do you have anything to suck on?"

"Sure." She reached into a side pocket of her swollen tote bag and produced a honey-flavored lozenge.

He turned his head to her. "Are you okay?"

"Well, yes, overall. I'm feeling so many emotions."

"Such as?"

"Surprise. Relief. Tenderness." She glanced upwards. "Anger. Resentment. You name it, I'm probably feeling it." Something else occurred to her. "How are you doing after this meeting?"

"Mostly relieved. Let's also throw in shell-shocked."

They sat quietly for a long moment. She could do this, working part time at the Center, out of her wheelhouse of strengths, rather than her administrative weaknesses. She could get up earlier each morning and devote an hour or two to the book project, go to work, and maybe even arrange her schedule so she had a day off to devote to her home and her mother's needs. She would, of course, need to discuss her travel schedule with Derek and pray he understood she wasn't as free to roam the country as he was.

"Paul?"

"Yes?"

"How did Craig react?"

He lifted his hand from the steering wheel. "I can't say he was happy, that's for sure. He sulked a good bit over not getting precisely what he wanted for once in his life."

"Do you think you made an enemy?" The thought stuck like a burr in her spirit.

"I didn't make a friend, but then there was strength in numbers tonight. Those people have a high regard for you, and a good bit of affection."

Erin leaned back into the comfortable car seat, allowing herself to relax, breathing in, breathing out. Like her Grandfather Peter in the Musch episode, her peers had vindicated her. Like was just about perfect. And she'd had nothing to do with it.

CHAPTER TEN

He'd been near here before. With a driving rainstorm bearing down on him and Pastor Rodenheimer, Peter's memories kept him company in lieu of conversation or reading a new letter from his remaining brother, one initially delivered to Peter, Jr.'s home, while slogging through Sussex County farmlands. Five years earlier, he'd led Northampton County's First Battalion across New Jersey toward a lopsided but noble fight against the British on the Brooklyn Heights. What was left of his command had endured a brutal season of captivity, then were released in February 1777 when Peter was paroled to his home in Easton. The journey back came at the worst time of year, with bruising cold and virulent winds inflicting themselves on his ill-clad, starving men, doggedly willing themselves back to homes and hearths. He recalled the small kindnesses of farmers allowing them the comfort of a barn in which to bed down at night or a handful of apples to stay their hollow stomachs. They'd barely managed to keep Conrad Fartenius, one of Easton's stablers, alive, no easy task given treacherous weather and his emaciated state.

Peter lifted a handkerchief to his face and wiped away wind-driven raindrops, unable to clear his spirit of the memories. He was grateful each of the men had been reunited with their families, recalling the joyous cries of women and children, the gentle backslapping and handshakes from male villagers, the ministrations of food and shelter at the church-turned-into-a- hospital. He sighed. Fartenius had convalesced for a year after their return, and over the following two, had been able to run his business, assisted by his wife Christina and their daughter. This past January, however, he'd contracted a respiratory illness his compromised body could not shake, and now he lay under the oaks at the German Reformed Cemetery.

This sojourn through New Jersey brought its own share of suspense, but he managed to evade fear. Just before leaving, he'd told Catherine, "a person doesn't plan to carry out evil at a church. If the writer of the letter had intended harm, he would have suggested a tavern or a home or along the road at a designated location. Not a house of God."

The memory of his wife bowing her head in agreement, her hand pressed to her heart, had relieved him of his deepest concern. The words of assurance had found their mark.

The rain persisted throughout most of the twenty-six mile journey, and by the time Peter and the minister arrived in German Valley, the sun was slipping past the western horizon. He and Rodenheimer checked into a respectable-looking tavern and quickly changed into dry garments, laying their wet clothes over chairs and the bed, pulling them closer to the fireplace. Peter reached into his leather satchel and exhaled with relief to find Charles's letter dry and safe. He tucked it in his waist coat and, fetching his reed pipe, followed Rodenheimer downstairs where the husband and wife owners set a hearty repast, with a table adjacent to the fireplace.

The rotund man placed his hands on the back of his hips. "You came from Easton?"

"Yes."

"You had a long trip then. What can I get you to drink?"

Peter deferred to his companion. "Pastor?"

"I would enjoy some tea."

"And for you, sir?"

"I'll have the same."

The man sauntered away, and Rodenheimer offered to give thanks, which he carried out with uncustomary brevity. The men dug into their venison stew and shared a loaf of rye bread. Once they'd taken the edge off their hunger, they commenced eating more slowly. Peter inclined his left arm toward the heat to reduce the perpetual ache he'd experienced on the road.

"I regret we were unable to talk much as we traveled," Rodenheimer finally said. "We had a good deal to discuss and little opportunity with the wind and rain blowing at us."

Peter closed his eyes and nodded his head. In truth, he didn't feel much like talking now either. He'd prefer lighting his pipe and reading his brother's letter.

"Hopefully tomorrow's weather will be much more favorable as we meet your correspondent."

"You say you know the minister of this Lutheran church where the rendezvous is to take place."

"I met him once, a few years ago while you were in New York. He served in the Continental Army and visited his soldiers at our church. Name of Muhlenberg."

Peter gazed into the leaping flames. "I wonder why the letter writer chose the church, here."

"I've been puzzling over that myself."

He smiled at Rodenheimer. "We shall find out tomorrow."

The minister had excused himself shortly after the evening meal and gone to their room, inadvertently granting Peter his wish for a solitary spell. Though decades younger, Rodenheimer wasn't used to rugged demands on his body, and the thought gave Peter a certain solace in his own, more advanced, years. He reached for his spectacles and his brother's letter, leaned into the Windsor chair, and puffed on his pipe.

October 8, 1781
My Dear Brother,
May this letter find you and your dear family

in peace and enjoying good health. Susanna and our noisy brood are doing well, as are our cherished mother and our departed brother Andrew's family. The harvest is keeping most of us busy, although my fellow citizens apparently thought I was not engaged enough to satisfy them. You see, they have elected me to the Pennsylvania Assembly, and I am humbled and honored to be following you, dear brother, in your footsteps.

Peter rested the letter on his lap, grinning to himself. Charles would make an excellent legislator, of that Peter was confident, knowing Charles's measured way of gathering and carefully considering information before allowing himself to make any decisions, in addition to his calm and principled aspect. The citizens of the upper part of Bucks County had chosen well. Of course, such service took much time away from home life and obligations, so Susanna and their older children would need to step up as well. Peter gazed into the fire before he returned to the letter.

Although I have not served in the military as you and Andrew have done at such great cost, you have always had my deepest support and my ongoing prayers. Now I will have an opportunity to sit among other publicly favored men to guide the course of our commonwealth's new government. I have promised to do so to the utmost of my human abilities, aided by our unfailing Lord. I will count on you to pray for your brother, that I may serve as faithfully as you and Andrew and thus bring further honor to our family.

Have you been kept busy as Northampton County's Lieutenant? Knowing you as I do, you continue to sacrifice time and resources in service to God, Home, and Country.

Peter came to the end of the letter, his eyelids beginning to droop as he petitioned the Almighty for Charles, for the Assembly, and for his own wisdom come the break of tomorrow's new day.

The man who'd come out of the stone church to greet them thrust out a hand the size of a ham hock as he strode up to Peter and Rodenheimer. Thankfully, the day had dawned bright, chilly, and clear, and by the early afternoon the foliage had shaken free of the previous day's downpour, shimmering its vibrant treasures.

"Good day gentleman! I am Deitrich Schmidt, Lutheran pastor of the Union Church."

Peter glanced sideways at his companion.

Rodenheimer reached the man first and pumped his hand in greeting. "Good day. I am Martin Rodenheimer of the German Reformed Church in Easton, Pennsylvania, and this is my friend, Colonel Peter Kichline."

"Good day, Pastor." Peter reached out his hand.

"Good day."

"I must confess I expected to see a Mr. Muhlenberg," Rodenheimer said.

Schmidt pursed his lips. "Yes, yes. He was the pastor here for a short while and is now with the Continental Army, a fighting parson if you will."

Peter quietly let this bit of news sink in, wondering if the change would make any difference to them.

"Ah, well, how nice to make your acquaintance," Rodenheimer said.

"What brings you to these parts?"

Rodenheimer gave his companion a "take-it-from-here" look, and Peter stepped forward, explaining their purpose in coming. He ended by showing the summoning letter to Schmidt, who took several minutes studying the lone page. "Does any of this seem familiar to you?"

"No, I'm afraid not." He handed the letter back to Peter. "What do you think this might be about?"

"Frankly, I do not know."

Schmidt's brow wrinkled. "Have you considered this might be a trap?"

"My wife has." Peter allowed himself a grim smile. "However, I do not think a trap is likely."

"I have nothing immediate to attend to. Would you like to come inside and wait?"

Peter briefly considered the invitation. "Thank you, but I prefer to wait here, at least for now. If this person fails to come within the hour, I will tarry inside. Perhaps Mr. Rodenheimer would like to go into the church?"

Schmidt waved a hand toward the stone building. "Come, my friend. "

"I should very much like to explore your beautiful building."

The men disappeared inside, and Peter began wishing he had brought his horse rather than walked, feeling exposed as he stood there, even in uniform. He visually examined his environment, then after taking an exploratory walk around the grounds, rested on a wooden bench under a fiery oak. *The temperature must be in the forties. I could use a mug of hot coffee.* He considered how he could go back to the tavern and secure the beverage, then return to the church within ten minutes, but Peter didn't want to risk missing his party. He spent the next half hour reading from the small Bible he'd once carried into battle, alternately praying and absorbing the grandeur of such a fine autumn day. At one point he began to nod off, having suffered the effects of disjointed sleep in a strange place with a bedfellow whose snoring could have powered Peter's sawmill.

Just before two o'clock, his ears pricked at the sound of horse's hooves in the near distance. A lone rider appeared over the swell of a hill, heading toward the church. *This must be him.* He lifted his flattened right hand to just above his eyebrows as if employing a field glass until his eyes met those of the horseman, who drew near and dismounted.

"Good day, sir. Colonel Kichline if I am not mistaken?"

Securing the animal to a hitching post. Peter studied the man, of average height, though rather large overall, guessing him to be somewhere in his thirties or early forties. Something about him seemed familiar.

Peter extended his hand. "A good day to you. Yes, I am Colonel Kichline."

"I must say, you are looking far better than the last time I saw you."

Peter dipped his chin, studying the face as they shook hands. "Then we've met?"

"Yes, I'm Pastor Aaron Burton of Trinity Church in New York."

A fluttering filled his stomach. "Are you not the pastor of the church where my men and I were imprisoned?"

Burton crossed his arms over his chest. "The very same. And how are you, and your men?"

Peter exhaled with the realization this benevolent man, whatever his purpose, bore no danger or ill will. But why him? Why now? He found his voice again. "I am quite well, thank you. My men suffered greatly, but all but one who was with me at the church have survived and are at home in Easton."

He sighed. "What a bad time you had of things, but I am grateful for those who returned to their families." He gazed at Peter. "Well, then, no doubt you're wondering what is going on here."

Peter gave a laugh, lightened somewhat by the man's breezy manner. "The thought has crossed my mind. You have come a very long way."

Burton pointed toward the bench. "May we have a seat?"

The men took their places at opposite ends, facing each other, and the pastor picked up the reigns of conversation. "I'll get right to the point, Colonel. I'm here on behalf of Mrs. Major Greta Hough."

Peter's breath caught. "Greta?"

"Yes, sir."

"Whatever for? Is she in trouble?"

"Mrs. Hough finds herself in a tenuous position and tells me she has no one else she believes she can turn to."

Conversation spilled from the church door, and the two other ministers immediately joined them, Peter making introductions. Then he said, "Pastor Burton, allow me to provide some details before you begin." He turned toward Rodenheimer and Schmidt. "The woman on whose behalf he has come was, along with her widowed father, indentured to me in Easton some twenty years ago. Shortly after my first wife died, Greta, whose last name was then Schmidt, married a British captain and moved first to Philadelphia, then to New York. While I was imprisoned there, my men and I initially were detained at the church Pastor Burton serves. At that time, Captain, excuse me, Major Hough, encountered me and secretly provided a better allotment of food for us. After I was permitted to stay under house arrest in a private home, Mrs. Hough often brought me provisions, and when I was allowed to return to Easton on parole, she supplied my men and me with a wagon, a horse, food, and blankets."

Schmidt exhaled as if he'd been holding his breath the entire time.

Burton picked up the reins of the story. "Mrs. Hough finds herself in a rather compromised position and believes Colonel Kichline can guide her." He gazed toward the distant hills while a squirrel scurried past the men and raced up a tree. "She has had no word from her husband in several months. He was sent south with his regiment roughly a year ago, and he wrote her on a regular basis. The letters have stopped coming. Mrs. Hough has made ceaseless inquiries, but she doesn't know whether the major is dead or alive, a prisoner of war, or perhaps in a hospital."

Peter stared at his weather-beaten hands, stirred by the difficulty of her plight.

"The British command has informed her, along with all the other officers' wives, they must put their affairs in order and evacuate New York as soon as possible. Mrs. Hough has two choices— she can go to England and live with her husband's family or relocate to Canada where the British will help establish displaced spouses and children."

The memory of her with the British officers' wives from a long ago encounter on a Philadelphia Street where they had taunted his German heritage loomed before him. Peter couldn't imagine Greta going to England and living with the Houghs, who surely must be a family of some means to have produced an army officer. Even if the Houghs did take her and the children—he thought there might be three of them—out of obligation to their son, Greta might never be treated civilly.

"She finds herself in a difficult situation. What has she decided?" Rodenheimer asked.

"Mrs. Hough believes there might be another possibility, and that is why I am here today as her emissary. She thought coming here herself would have been too risky. Colonel." He turned to Peter. "This is where you come in."

"Do continue." His left calf tingled.

"She would very much like to return home to her father and live once again in Easton where she says she was quite contented. However, she doesn't know if he will welcome her because of her connection to the British. I understand Mr. Schmidt didn't have much contact with her after the war began."

Peter didn't know whether they had or not, but Hans Schmidt had never had a bad word for his daughter at any time. "As far as I know, Mrs. Hough's father has no ill will toward her."

"That is good to know." Burton paused, looking up into the cloud dusted sky. "Of course, even if her father welcomes her and the children, would they be accepted, or more importantly, safe from reprisal in Easton? She says she would maintain a low profile, but she doesn't know if being married to a British officer would go badly for them."

Ah, that was the rub.

CHAPTER ELEVEN

"Oh, I'm so very glad to be back in your good graces." Connie Pierce leaned forward and covered Erin's hand with her own. "I've been all torn apart about this unpleasantness."

Erin's eyes misted. "I feel the same way. What Craig did against me is understandable from his power-grabbing point of view, but to separate good friends ..."

"Before we put this behind us, I want to assure you I never agreed with his scheme to put me in charge of the Kichline Center. I was happy to oversee the renovation, to lend a hand, but I always considered this a temporary arrangement."

"I know. In my heart, I believed this to be true. Although I was upset, I wanted to give you the benefit of any doubts I had." She squeezed, then released, Connie's hand. "I just couldn't see you as part of Craig's little fiefdom."

At ear level, she batted her hands against the air. "Oh, that man!"

Toby commenced a loud snoring at Erin's feet, and the women laughed, then smiled at each other.

"I have an idea for the grand opening," Erin said.

"Oh, I can't wait!" Connie gave a little bounce. "Tell me."

"How about if I get Derek McCutcheon to speak at the dedication?"

She nearly shot out of her chair. "Erin! Do you think he would? Oh, what a coup that would be! Take that, Craig Reldan!"

Erin smiled at her friend's delight. "I'm certainly going to try. After that mess in Chicago, he owes me." She chuckled. "Well, not exactly owes me, but I think he'd be open to coming."

"Would he be terribly expensive, though?"

"I'm not sure what he charges, but remember, this is a Lafayette College project, and they get world class speakers on a regular basis."

"Of course you're right. I don't know why I didn't think about that."

"When do you think the Center will be ready?" Erin asked.

She tapped her fingertips on the table. "We've had a few delays with the HVAC system, but we're back on track now, and I think we're looking at possibly February, March at the latest."

"Well, then, I'd better get cracking with a program for the opening, along with exhibits and a line-up of other speakers."

"I don't know how you do everything you do, Erin. You amaze me."

"I don't know, since I'm not teaching, my life is a lot more manageable. I can write the books and curate the Center, just not the books, the Center, and teaching."

"What about traveling? Does Mr. McCutcheon expect you to do much?"

"I'm not sure," she admitted. "I need to discuss his expectations with him. As for me, I think I can manage monthly, but any more would really stretch me."

"How does Paul feel about your being on the road ... and Ethan?"

Erin squirmed. This part of her writing life was all so new, but one thing she did know—they came first. She just hoped Derek agreed. "They didn't have any issues with my going to Chicago, but we need to talk about what's realistic for us long-term."

"Yes, of course. If I can help out while you're on the road, just let me know. I'd be willing to drive Ethan where he needs to go or make a meal or check on your mom."

Erin's jaw dropped. "You would?"

"What are friends for, right?"

"Yes, but ..."

"I'm enjoying sitting back and watching just how high you can fly."

The words shimmered over Erin, a benediction to their reunion after the debacle, and her spirit newly freed, she suddenly remembered what she'd been dying to share with Connie. "That means a lot to me. Now then, there's something amazing I have to show you."

Erin hustled to her office, grabbed her ancestor's journal and the white curator gloves, and went back to the kitchen where she held the book at her friend's eye level.

Connie gasped, pointing. "What is this?"

"This is my grandfather Peter's diary from 1781."

"What!"

Erin's heart almost burst with pride as she told her friend about its discovery in a church vault and what she was discovering about her ancestor's life during that period.

"Oh, may I?"

Erin handed the gloves to her friend, who wriggled her hands into them. Connie picked up and cradled the centuries-old book as if it were a newborn. "I just can't believe this. What a find!"

"After I finish my translating, I am hoping the church will let the Center display this as a tribute to its namesake."

"What a great idea! We could build an exhibit about him." Her excitement built. "Oh, Erin, maybe we can find some other local, eighteenth century diaries." Connie's hand flew to her mouth. "Oh, listen to me, trying to do your job!"

Erin laughed. "And you said you weren't after it!"

As they shared a light moment, the garage door began sliding open, and Erin heard Paul pulling his car inside, awakening their slumbering dog. A moment later, the door slammed, rattling the frame, and he entered the house. He stopped in his tracks as he neared the kitchen and, eyes sweeping the scene, he grinned. Toby wandered over to him, and Paul bent down to rub the dog's head.

"Am I ever glad to see you two together again."

Ethan yawned and stretched, then rose from the sofa in the family room where an episode of

"The Clone Wars" had just ended. "I think I'll go up now."

Erin checked her watch—eight-thirty. "Be sure to take a shower and to wash your neck and ears."

"Oh, Mom. You know I do."

He stomped upstairs without a "good-night," and Erin decided she'd give him time to sulk and shower before performing a stealth version of tucking him in. As if following her cue, Paul also remained silent. She wondered how much time would pass before they worked seamlessly together on the niggling details of raising Ethan. Paul had been in charge on a few occasions, but when they were together, he naturally defaulted to Erin. She was hoping for more of a balance. She'd shared this desire with her new husband, who agreed she had a strong point, and they pledged to work toward that goal. For now, however, she understood there needed to be a time of transition, and transitions with stepchildren were delicate things.

As if Ethan's yawn had been contagious, Paul reared back his upper body and covered his mouth.

"Not you too?" Erin teased him.

"Yes, me too. I could easily fall asleep just now, but I don't want to abandon you."

She perked up. "Actually you'd be doing me a favor."

"What?"

"Don't look so shocked. I'm dying to get back into Grandfather Peter's diary, and I'm not a bit sleepy."

He rose and lifted her right hand. "Well then, my lady, I leave you in good hands." Toby raised his head from his supine position. "And yours, good sir." Kissing her hand, he then leaned over and pressed his lips against Erin's, lingering. When he broke away, she watched as he ascended the stairs and disappeared around the corner, savoring the impression of his kiss and his attractive form.

"Well, Toby, it's you and me then. Want to come to my office?"

The basset pricked his ears, stretched, then followed her.

Erin opened the journal to the entry dated October 16, 1781. "What is it about that date?" she asked aloud. Toby perked up, then lowered his head to his paws. "Of course! The surrender at Yorktown was right around the corner, October 19th." She fought an urge to read ahead, eager to know what her ancestor had to say on that auspicious day, wondering how, and where, he had observed the event. "Then again, he wouldn't have known on the day the surrender took place. News would have taken several days to reach Laston. Ah well, sir Toby, I shall read on!" She opened her computer to the translation function and began the meticulous work of transcribing Peter's words. She plodded through sections of nearly invisible ink, her pace tortoise-like. The first few lines took twenty minutes.

German Valley, NJ
This must be brief as I will leave the inn as soon as Mr. Rodenheimer collects his belongings

and the pastor who represented my mysterious letter writer refreshes himself and his horse.

"A pastor! I wonder why a pastor got involved." Erin blinked to moisten her eyes and continued reading.

> Mr. Aaron Burton shepherds the church in which I and some of my men were detained just after the Battle of Brooklyn. He is a godly man who is here on behalf of Greta Hough, nee Schmidt.

"A woman wrote that letter, Toby! This wasn't a military matter at all. Grandfather Peter seems to know who she was." Her left calf tingled.

> Greta lived with my family some twenty years ago when she and her father Hans came from Germany as indentured servants. Toward the end of their tenure, she received a proposal of marriage from a British captain, Stephen Hough, who was stationed in our area. I last encountered them in New York. Major Hough found me in a pitiable condition at the hospital in the church and secretly arranged for me and my men to receive more provisions. Greta supplied many of our needs in the following months, including for our long journey home. Her husband went with the army to the southern campaigns some time ago and has not been heard from in many weeks. The British command have told her she must go with them to Canada with the other officers' families, or they will arrange transport to England, so she may live with her in-laws.

Erin blew out a puff of air and, standing up to stretch, considered the acute nature of this Greta's decision. Either way, she would be in unknown territory. She wondered whether a simple servant who'd married well had ever truly fit in with the other officers and their wives. As class-based as British society was, life could have been challenging, even on her home turf, let alone in England. Erin thought back to the poorly-executed letter the woman had written to her ancestor, indicating the most basic literacy. She gazed at a flickering candle she'd lit over an hour ago, wondering what she would have done in the woman's shoes then sat back down and picked up the diary. She was prepared to stay up all night if necessary, although her morning writing session would surely suffer after putting in the long hours.

> With no one else she felt she could trust and having a different path in mind, she asked Pastor Burton to meet me on her behalf— coming straight to me would have been far too risky. She would like me to speak to her father and his wife, to see if they would take in her and her three children. She would very much like to return to Easton, which she still thinks of as home. Mr. Burton will take Hans Schmidt's response back to Greta with all due haste, so she may know what to do. The three of us must depart for Easton at once because the British likely will be pulling out of New York soon.

Erin reached the end of the entry, her heart aching for the unfortunate wife and mother, who seemed pressed in on all sides. She placed the journal carefully on the side table and wandered to the kitchen for a bottle of water. Finding a piece of leftover salmon, she poured chocolate sauce over it and ate standing up while hoping Greta did return to Easton. But would she have been accepted after being married to a British officer and moving in and among Loyalists in New York? Greta might be shunned in the little village. She swallowed the last bites of her snack and returned to her office to continue squinting at—and translating—the faded writing.

> October 18, 1781
> What a busy few days these have been! I shall long remember the expression on the face of Hans Schmidt as Pastor Burton revealed Greta's condition and explained his purpose in coming to Easton. Both Hans and his wife took no time at all to respond. As one, they told Mr. Burton to bring Greta and her children, heedless of any consequences. This is their daughter, and they want her home. Nearly as soon as the words had come out of Hans's mouth, Pastor Burton was back in his saddle. Catherine and I will do what we can to reacclimate them.

"Hooray!" Erin called out, then slapped her hand to her mouth. The last thing she wanted was to make Toby howl at this hour. She checked her watch and gave a start—one-twenty-six. She put the diary in her desk drawer, turned off the computer, and took Toby out before heading upstairs. In the cold, clear night, the half-moon casting its spell over the river, and through the city lights, she made out the hazy outline of the Big Dipper. She hoped for Greta and her children's sake, all really ended well that seemed to start well.

CHAPTER TWELVE

The appearance of Colonel Kichline and his companions had drawn each member of the Schmidt family to the farm's entrance. Following a particularly successful indentured service, Schmidt had created a successful dairy farm a mile upstream from the mills with his devoted wife and a quiverfull of children, seven at last count. Each of them spoke a curious blend of English, German, and Leni Lenape, due to the heritage of Schmidt's second wife, who went by the name Mary, although Hans persisted in using her Lenape "Silver Cloud," which he often said in German, *Ginster-Holzrindeneule.*

Watching the scene unfold, Peter considered an ironic twist to this family's story: Hans Schmidt didn't speak his wife's language, nor did Mary understand more than the most basic German or English. Back in 1766 when she met—and married—her British captain, Greta's English was faltering at best. Although father and daughter had acquired a passing knowledge of English over the years, love seemed to possess its own means of communication.

Seeing his three visitors, Schmidt wiped his hands on the sides of his pant legs as he headed toward them. *"Guten tag, Herr Kichline, Herr Rodenheimer!"*

"Guten tag!" Peter dismounted and wrapped the reins around a fence post while the pastor followed suit. Burton dismounted but stayed close to his mare.

An explosion of noise pierced the air as children from toddlerhood to adolescence surged toward them, accompanied by the syncopated barking of their friendly dogs. Mrs. Schmidt emerged from the house holding a baby and smiled in Peter's direction. His spirit filled with joy at the sight of the large, robust brood. *Greta and her children could be happy here, although Providence knows where they will all sleep.*

Peter introduced Pastor Burton, who lost no time telling Greta's story or the purpose of his visit, Peter translating as needed. Before Burton had reached the conclusion, Peter noted the way Schmidt was looking at his wife with pursed lips and a firm jaw.

"I wish for *Meine Tochter* to come," he said. "You will tell her, *ja?*"

Peter spoke up. "Yes, straightaway. Understand, Hans, not everyone may be as welcoming as you are."

"Ja, ja." Schmidt waved his hand as if at a gnat. *"Sie ist meine Familie, mein Fleisch und mein Blut."*

Peter glanced at Mary Schmidt, giving silent ascent with a firm nodding of her head. "Mr. Burton, they very much want her and the children to live here."

"His message was quite understandable even to me. And so, if you will excuse me, I will commence my ride back to New York this very minute." He climbed up on his horse.

"Excuse me, but might you want a fresh mount?" Peter asked.

Burton shook his head. "There's no time to lose. I'll rest him along the way and make sure to give him a proper recovery at home."

"Thank you." Peter reached up to shake his hand. "You have put your own safety in jeopardy, and I pray God to spare you any unpleasantness. If you like, I can send someone to ride back with you, one of my sons or workers."

"Thank you for the kind offer, but again, I must not hesitate." Burton tipped his cap to Peter, Rodenheimer, and the Schmidts, and he rode off.

"Oh, hello, Mr. Traill." Catherine skidded to a halt as she sailed down the hallway bearing an armful of bed linens.

Robert Traill stood and gave a bow, and Peter also rose from his chair near the warming fire. "Good day, Mrs. Kichline. I see you are quite employed."

"Do please sit down." She looked from him to her husband. "Does he know about Greta?"

Peter lifted his chin. "Yes, I was just telling him."

"And when do you expect her arrival?" Traill asked.

"I had a message yesterday from Pastor Burton, who is assisting her. She hopes to be in Easton in a day or two."

"What a tricky business," his friend said.

"Bett and I have been gathering bed linens from our own stores, and your Elizabeth has also contributed, Mr. Traill. I'm guessing Greta won't be able to bring very much with her at the risk of detection. Well, then, I must get back to work. Good day."

"Good day, Mrs. Kichline." Traill looked over at Peter as they settled back into their comfortable chairs. "How will Mrs. Hough get out without being seen?"

Peter puffed on his pipe before answering. "When the children leave school, they will go to the pastor's house instead of home, then Greta will follow in the evening."

The sound of Catherine and Bett conferring together drifted down the hall from the dining room. Peter smelled bread baking, his favorite of all scents. Bread, not biscuits. He'd never gotten used to those little round cakes which he considered the worst kind of yeastless imposters.

Traill frowned. "The plan is full of holes, Peter. How will she pack her belongings into the wagon? Women don't travel lightly you know. Besides, how will she manage a journey across New Jersey by herself?"

"William Carpenter volunteered to help and, in fact, left earlier this morning. He's going to meet them a few miles into New Jersey, where Pastor Burton will drop them off."

Peter couldn't tell why his friend was getting so tied up in knots over the situation, a man who normally towered with strength. He risked a gentle rebuke. "I would beg you to remember in whose care we all are, my friend."

Traill raked a hand through his thatch of hair. "I deserved that. Sometimes my stubborn practicality pushes to the side my spiritual understanding. We are called to walk by faith, not sight."

Peter reached over and patted his friend's knee. "I am afflicted with the same malady."

They rested a bit from conversation, enjoying the peaceful understanding between them and the homey ambience.

"Good heavens!" Peter jumped from his seat when someone began pounding the front door, seemingly with both fists.

"I think I just jumped out of my skin!" Traill placed his right hand over his heart.

"What in the world?" Catherine rushed down the hallway, Joe and Bett on her tail.

Peter reached the door first and flung it open to see the beet red face of Private Fowler Massey, who acted as a courier for Robert Levers. The young man's brown eyes appeared ready to pop under his tricorn which barely covered a mass of untidy white-blonde hair. "Private Massey!" He looked down to see a copy of *The Freeman's Journal* in the fellow's hand, which was trembling.

Massey opened his mouth, puffing from his exertion. "Colonel Kichline, sir, I came here first." More puffing. "Just came. From Philadelphia. Look!" With an inelegant flourish he unfolded and thrust the paper into Peter's hands.

He tried to focus on the blur before him, feeling a growl rise in his chest when he realized he didn't have his reading glasses.

His friend reached for the paper. "May I?"

"Yes, of course."

Traill let out a long whistle.

Catherine clutched her hands. "What is it, Mr. Traill?"

"I've never seen the likes of this before," he said. "There is big news, and they've put it right on the front page, not on the inside as usual."

"What does it say?" She was all but panting.

He held the paper at arm's length and read aloud. "'Be it remembered! That on the 19th day of October, 1781, Lieut. General Charles Earl Cornwallis, with above 5,000 British troops, surrendered themselves prisoners of war to his Excellency Gen. George Washington, commander in chief of the allied forces of France and America. Laus Deo!'"

"Oh! Oh!" Catherine clapped her right hand to her breast. "Does this mean ...?"

"Is de war over?" Bett's voice carried a slight moan.

Peter's left calf tingled, then traveled all the way up to the roots of his thinning hair. "What is the date on the paper?"

"Let's see. October 24th."

"Yesterday." He turned to Massey. "You just brought this from Philadelphia?"

"Yes, sir, hot off the presses. Normally, I deliver the paper to Colonel Levers then to you." He lowered his voice. "Somehow, I wanted you to see this first, though Mr. Levers will be none too happy with me."

Peter put his hand on the young man's shoulder, the only thing keeping him from either grabbing the paper to read the details or running headlong down Northampton Street as a self-appointed town crier. "I appreciate it." He was about to ask Bett for his hat and coat, only to find she was already standing there holding them out to him, beaming ear-to-ear. Before taking off with the men, he knew the occasion called for a different gesture altogether. He walked over to his wife and gazed lovingly into her eyes as he squeezed her hands.

"Oh, darling, is it really true?" A tear slipped down her cheek, and he brushed it away with his thumb.

"I do believe so."

"May I tell anyone else?"

"No, my dear. The news must not go further than this house. Let's give Mr. Levers a chance to announce the glad tidings to the village. I think we owe that to him."

"Yes, of course. Oh, but I want to shout from the housetops!"

He smiled at her. "I promise you, there will be a celebration such as Easton has never seen before. In the meantime, wait for the town crier."

As expected, Robert Levers scowled over his courier's breaking the momentous news to Peter first, but his outward jubilation over the British surrender broke through his vexation with Massey. "Oh joyous day!'

Mrs. Levers and the rest of his staff rushed into the parlor talking all at once—"What is it?" "What has happened?"

Levers broke into his most pompous posture, pumping his hands. "Quiet all! Let's be quiet. Now then, I have just received news from Philadelphia." He paused, as if for dramatic effect. "The British have surrendered to General Washington at Yorktown, Virginia!"

"Huzzah!"

"Hip hip huzzah!"

"Praise the Almighty!"

When the hubbub died down after several minutes of shouting and hats being thrust into the air, Peter noticed a crowd was gathering at the front door. Looking at Levers, he jerked his head in an invitation for a private word.

Levers came over and clapped him on the shoulder. "Oh, what a joyous day my friend! At times I thought we'd never receive such cheering news."

"It is a time for celebration indeed."

"You wanted a word?"

Peter nodded his head. "The village needs to be told straightaway. A crowd has already formed." He looked toward the front door, and Levers followed his gaze, then pursed his lips.

"We must gather at the Courthouse as we did on July 8, 1776. Let's say three o'clock. That gives us two hours to prepare, and hopefully we can keep the news secret until then. How quickly can you gather your remaining men?"

"With assistance, I can have them at the courthouse by that time." Peter rocked on the back of his heels. "Before moving forward, I suggest you and I consult the newspaper for details. A headline will only take us so far."

"You are right, of course, Colonel Kichline." He waved Massey over to where they stood. "Mr. Massey, I want you to find Alexander Porter, the town crier. Tell him to announce a three o'clock meeting at the Great Square." Glowering, he thrust his face toward his personal courier. "You are not to breathe a word of the news to a soul, do you understand?"

"Yes, sir!"

"Now then, be on your way." He backed away and addressed Peter and Robert Traill. "Would you gentlemen care to examine the contents of the news?"

They savored the details as if a fine meal—the Americans, aided by the French, had pounded the British with their heaviest artillery, then stormed several redoubts, followed by a short burst of hand-to-hand fighting. With their cannons poised nearly at point-blank range of the British, General Cornwallis employed the same tactic that had saved Washington's remaining forces at Brooklyn—a furtive evacuation across the river by night. This time, however, Providence did not favor the fleeing soldiers. With a third of the men safely across the York River, a sudden storm drove the men and their boats scattershot downriver. Cornwallis ordered those who had been able to cross to return, but the unfortunate men came under grueling fire. By noon, the British general was waving a white flag. He refused, in the end, to surrender personally to General Washington, sending an aide to the task, claiming Cornwallis was indisposed. Washington, in turn, sent his own deputy to receive the British general's sword as the defeated army's musicians played "The World Turned Upside Down."

Peter stared at the paper, breathless, as if he had personally been present at the beginning of the end of British rule over the new and independent United States of America. And so, in a way, he had been. Start to finish.

"Wow." Traill muttered as he reached the end of the report.

Levers expelled a dramatic sigh. "A great day indeed. A very great day."

"The British are still occupying some of our ports," Traill said. "I don't mean to throw water on this good news, but we'll have to figure some things out before a treaty can be signed."

Peter agreed. "Yes, but we can still celebrate having won this great contest."

Puffing out his chest, Levers addressed his comrade. "Colonel Kichline, on that day five years ago I announced to the village a Declaration of Independence. Will you do the honor today of proclaiming the end of the war?"

He stared into Lever's dark eyes, wordlessly giving assent when his voice failed him.

Processing toward the Great Square on horseback, accompanied by a fifer and drummer, Peter gazed at the gathering of upturned faces, reading in their expressions a state of being on emotional tiptoes. Why the pageantry? Was this an occasion for good news or bad? What needed to be told to the entire village, rather than disseminated through the grapevine beginning with Meyer Hart's store? Even the pigs had ceased their energetic foraging under the crimsoned trees by the courthouse pond.

Following Peter were Levers, Traill, and a host of current duty military and veterans marching on foot. How he'd rejoiced at the sight of Isaac Sidman, Peter Horn, Peter Horeback, Michael Gress, and John Spangenberg falling into the line, each wearing a sprig of green in their tricorns, just as they had at Brooklyn when uniforms were in short supply. Peter squinted through the blazing sun at his female family members, his sons marching with him in the haphazard column.

When the parade came to a halt, his commanding presence extinguished individual conversations as one snuffs out candles. Peter went to the top of the stairs, took a deep breath, then let his voice rise above a light breeze and the cawing of crows. "My fellow Eastonians, five years ago we gathered in this square to hear a Declaration of Independence which led us into a fight for our freedom from British tyranny. Over the course of those years we have, each of us, sacrificed much."

He swallowed around a swelling in his throat as he thought of Ziba Wiggins and Conrad Fartenius, spotting their widows and children in the throng.

"I bring you momentous news—on October 19th at Yorktown in Virginia, British General Cornwallis surrendered." He paused over the collective gasp. "My friends, the war is over!"

A spontaneous cry ascended to the heavens— "Hip hip huzzah! Hip hip huzzah! Hip hip huzzah!" Vigorous backslapping, embracing, hats tossed into the air, and not a few tears commenced. Peter watched, his chest filling with joy, and when the initial jubilation began to slow, he raised his hands to win back their attention.

"A celebration will begin with a service of Thanksgiving. Let us go to the house of God to thank Almighty God for this great victory."

"Hear the Word of God from Isaiah 59:18, 19. 'According to their deeds, accordingly he will repay, fury to his adversaries, recompence to his enemies; to the islands he will repay recompence. So shall they fear the name of the LORD from the west, and his glory from the rising of the sun. When the enemy shall come in like a flood, the Spirit of the LORD shall lift up a standard against him.'"

Pastor Rodenheimer's face bore a fierce joy, reflecting Peter's own emotions as he sat with his family. The last time the church had overflowed to this extent was as a hospital during the war—those memories forever imprinted on his mind.

"We rejoice with hymns of fervent praise," the minister preached, "because God has judged our enemies when we had no might against a great company that came against us and knew not what to do. Our eyes were upon him in our distress. We give glory to his name when he calls to mind that our most important successes, in almost every instance, have happened when we were peculiarly weak and distressed. Praise the Lord, for he is good, for his mercy endureth forever!"

Peter lifted his voice with the congregants: "Praise the Lord, for he is good, for his mercy endureth forever!"

CHAPTER THIRTEEN

Erin checked the time at the corner of her laptop—eight-fifteen. She'd been writing since Ethan left for school and Paul for a breakfast meeting with a client. Normally she would continue throughout the morning, but she needed to take her mom grocery shopping. In fact, with Thanksgiving in less than a week and the responsibility of hosting this year, she needed to put in her own supply of food, including a turkey. She rose and stretched. *If I leave in a half hour, I still have time to take Toby for a short walk around the campus.* She knew just the route, across Cattell Street to one of the side roads leading to Lafayette, then once around the Quad.

"C'mon, Toby." Her basset hound lumbered after her into the kitchen where she kept his leash on a hook by the door. "You're moving slower than usual today." Erin scanned his form, frowning. "I think my guys have been feeding you too many treats lately, and I haven't exactly been faithful about walking you. "

She snapped on the red leash then reached for her jacket and a pair of gloves. The weather had turned cold in the past two days, and the forecast called for a high of just forty-three degrees. She decided to wear her knit Lafayette cap. Outside Erin swished through leaf-covered sidewalks to the campus, their smokiness perfuming the atmosphere, pausing once for Toby to mark his spot. The sun proved a welcome counterpoint, and she walked faster to ward off the chill and to speed up her heart rate. She nodded greetings to a few students near the Farinon Center and at Hogg Hall said hello to one she'd had in one of her first classes there. At the library parking lot, however, she abruptly froze and grimaced, Toby trotting along until he strained at the end of the leash. Herman Weinreich was yukking it up with Craig Reldan near the latter's BMW M5. What really galled her was when Herman slapped his companion on the back. Her left eyelid twitching, she wheeled around to retrace her steps, not trusting herself to be in any way civil should they see her. *How dare Herman act like Craig is a regular guy and just the nicest person in Easton, instead of a first-rate rat!*

She had achieved a walking jog by the time she reached her front porch, unlocked the door, and released her anger in the safety of her living room. "Oooooo! That man gets under my skin!" Toby skittered down the hallway to safety. "I can't stand the sight of him." She slammed her gloves onto a console table. "I'll bet he spends more on his hair than his wife." Erin thudded to the kitchen where she yanked open the refrigerator door and pulled out a bottle of water. Drinking the cold liquid partially doused her red hot emotions, and followed by deliberate deep breathing, her emotional temperature began dialing back to normal. She didn't want to be in such a state when she picked up her mother. Erin knew she couldn't avoid bumping into Craig Reldan forever and would, in fact, be working with him on the Kichline Center board, but seeing him act all buddy-buddy with her beloved mentor had been as abrasive as showering with scouring powder.

"Are you sure you're all right?" Audrey may not have been able to see Erin's face clearly, but she certainly had eyes for the nether regions of her daughter's spirit.

"I'm fine, Mom, just focusing on which of these turkeys to buy." She poked a few of the fresh ones and raised her eyebrows over the price tags. Since when had turkeys become so expensive? "Isn't the rule a pound for every person?"

"It is. So, how many are you expecting again?"

They'd already covered this ground, at least three times. "Paul and his parents, Ethan, you and me, so six."

"What about Ethan's other grandparents?"

"I invited Pat and Al, but they haven't made up their minds just yet. Al recently had knee surgery and has been in a lot of pain."

"That's a real shame. They're nice people, and so are your new in-laws, although I haven't talked to them as much. Well, just in case, I think you should figure them in, and you'll want left overs."

She sighed. "I do wish Allen and the girls could be there, but they always do Thanksgiving with their in-laws."

As much as Erin would enjoy being with her brother and his family, cooking a feast for six was about all she felt she could manage.

Her mother brightened. "Just think, it's your first Thanksgiving with Paul."

"Yes, and I want the meal to be perfect, so don't let me forget anything. I left my list on my desk, and I won't have time to shop again before Louise and Tim arrive on Tuesday." She also needed to enlist Ethan and Paul in getting the house cleaned up. Lately, her upkeep had been slipping, and she didn't want there to be a particle of dust on furniture or a stray leaf on her floors.

"Don't worry, I'll help. I've made plenty of Thanksgiving meals in my day. You'll need potatoes, a big bag of russets. And cranberry sauce. And green beans." She paused. "Are you making that casserole?"

Erin shivered. "I can't stand that stuff. It's like swallowing little eels."

A look of wonder passed over Audrey's face. "How do you think of things like that?"

"Maybe because I'm a writer." She savored the taste of those words on her lips. She *was* a writer, and getting a lot of attention from her work with Derek McCutcheon. He'd recently emailed a review to her hailing her as a "fresh new voice in nonfiction."

"Well, then, we'll just have green beans, and how about carrots? You might want to roast them with the potatoes and then have mashed sweet potatoes. Of course, men like corn, so we'll need some of that, and are you baking pumpkin pies or buying them? They make good pies here."

"I think I'd like to make them myself." She wanted to impress her in-laws, but her head still spun. The perfect Thanksgiving dinner in the perfectly kept house required a lot of energy.

She had just finished putting fresh sheets on the guest room bed and laying out two sets of expertly folded towels when Ethan called out, "Mo-om, your phone's ringing!"

"I can hear it. I'll call back whoever it is."

"O-kay!"

Not only was her son's tread heavy these days, his voice had become louder and slightly deeper. She stepped back to examine the room, wondering whether or not she'd remembered to dust the blinds. A quick run of her index finger told her she had. When she went downstairs to the family room, Paul looked up from a new book about General Grant and reached for her hand. "Thank you for letting my parents come. I know it's a lot of work for you."

She bent over and kissed him. "I'm glad they're coming."

"Just let me know what I can do to help."

Ethan clumped over to them. "Mom, you'd better check and see who was calling you."

She mussed up his hair. "All right, Mr. Town Crier. I think I left the phone on the kitchen table."

She padded across the room in her sock feet and, checking her cell, discovered the caller had been Derek McCutcheon. She turned to the guys. "I'm going to my office. That was Derek."

"I wonder why he's calling on a Sunday night."

"Me too." She went to her room, settled into her recliner, and tapped "redial."

He answered after two rings. "Hello, my friend. Thank you for calling back so soon."

"I was upstairs, but my phone was not."

"How are you?"

She sensed he wasn't calling just to find out how she was. "I'm doing well—preparing the house for Thanksgiving. Paul's parents are coming up from Florida."

Something in the ensuing pause made her freeze.

"I see. Well, then, I think I may just cancel." He seemed to be talking to himself.

"Cancel? Cancel what?"

"I was scheduled to do an interview on Wednesday at the Boston flagship PBS station about the book, with a Thanksgiving theme, but, uh, well, you see we've had a bit of bad news from the doctor."

Her skin tingled. "Are you all right, Derek?"

"Yes, it's my wife, you see. She's just been diagnosed with lung cancer, and she's going in for surgery on Tuesday."

The words slammed into her consciousness, knowing first hand this kind of shellshock followed by months of being stretched on the rack physically and emotionally with no certain outcome. She brought her focus back to what Derek was saying.

"... many weeks of treatments. I'm afraid my plans are going to have to change for the foreseeable future. Our book deadline won't change as I'm pretty close to finished with my chapters, but I'm having to make several adjustments."

She pulled her Easton-themed throw around her, trembling. "I'm so sorry to hear your news, Derek."

"Yes, these things happen, as you well know."

Following a silent nod to their commonality, she spoke again, hoping she didn't come to regret asking, "What can I do to help?"

"I know how tight your calendar is, and of course, the holidays are upon our doorstep. However, if you can do any pinch hitting at all, well, there's the PBS show I just mentioned, then in two weeks, I have appearances in St. Louis and Dallas, and the week before Christmas, I am to host a holiday benefit in Atlanta."

She was free falling, imagining herself away from her family and home in crowded airports with Christmas music looping above the din of the hordes and endless announcements, her flights delayed, existing on caffeine and tabasco sauce to battle fatigue from not enough sleep.

She inhaled, then exhaled. Ready or not, here she came. "Which of these are the most important to you?"

"I would say the PBS show this week, and the benefit in Atlanta."

She ignored the part about "this week" and tackled the other one. "For a benefit, I'm guessing the organizers would want you and not a representative." She couldn't yet bring herself to refer to herself as his equal.

"You would do nicely, I'm sure, but I can check with them and get back to you." He paused. "I just had what I'm hoping you'll consider a rather good idea. You say your new in-laws and mother are coming for Thanksgiving, and you're hosting?"

"Yes."

"What if you come up to Boston to do the show? I mean, all of you come, my treat. I can fly everyone up there and throw in a Thanksgiving feast at Plimoth Plantation."

Erin wasn't the most spontaneous person on the planet, but even she was tempted to say "Yes please" before she could consult her family. What would they say to the sudden change? How much did they like, or dislike, surprises? She knew her mother wasn't too keen on them. Would they be terribly disappointed not to enjoy the holiday in Easton, or would they be up for an adventure that related to her work?

"Wow, Derek, that is very generous of you."

"Are you kidding? It's the very least I could do."

"Uh, isn't it a bit late to schedule a meal at Plimoth Plantation? They've probably been booked solid for months."

"Years actually. Not to worry. I have some connections, a favor to call in."

Of course he did.

"Let me check with my family and get back to you. Is tomorrow morning soon enough or do you need to know tonight?" She squirmed at the thought of saying "no" to *the* Derek McCutcheon, the renowned historian who'd given her to-die-for opportunities.

"Tomorrow morning is fine. And thank you for even considering this."

"You're very welcome. I'll be praying for you and Helen."

"I appreciate it."

She laid out the situation with Paul as they sat before the gas fireplace, Toby snoring at her feet, his body twitching from dreams probably of chasing squirrels. Her husband had listened without comment, a change from Jim, who used to jump in and out before she'd had a chance to finish. She reached out and touched his arm. "I'm ready for your feedback. You'll probably say Derek's idea about this week is out of the question, and I will more than understand. He's asking a lot."

Paul grinned. "I'm not going to say that at all. It's certainly inconvenient from the standpoint of all the plans we have in place, but then, illnesses are rarely convenient. You know what he and his wife are going through." He squeezed her hand. "So, if Ethan, my parents, and your mom go for the opportunity to spend Thanksgiving in Boston, is that what you want to do, to be on that show? And what about the other events he can't attend?"

The question she'd been kicking around for weeks without directly addressing had come upon her. She regarded him wide-eyed, marveling at the way he was able to detach his own self-interest to seek out what she wanted first. "I, uh, rather like the idea of getting further known as an author who's closely associated with Derek McCutcheon. The notoriety is satisfying, and while I'm comfortable giving speeches and doing appearances, the travel part isn't exactly fun or anywhere close to glamorous. I wouldn't mind a little, but he keeps a constant schedule, and honestly, I don't think I can handle what he does while writing and doing my Kichline Center job starting in a couple months, and being the wife, mother, and daughter I want to be. Then again, how can I say 'no' to Derek when I'm so very privileged to be working with him?"

"There is a lot to consider. First of all, though, you are not his acolyte. You are his partner, and though you're younger and have less experience, you're a doctor of history and an expert in your own right. You can meet him on level ground."

An inner light scattered the shadows. He was right. She needed to stop seeing herself in a subservient role with Derek because he was a celebrity.

Paul continued, looking into her eyes, melting her heart. "What do you want?"

She blurted, "I want to write books and do some appearances, but no more than once a month. And Paul, I can't do all of that and be there for my family and work even part time at the Kichline Center." She couldn't believe these words were coming out of her mouth, but she couldn't deny their veracity. "I think Connie should run the Center herself."

"Where did that come from?" Now he was wide-eyed.

She slumped back into the sofa, clapping her hand to her chest. "Wow, I wasn't expecting to say that. In Chicago, when I realized the job might be taken away from me, I came to understand as much as I loved the idea, I could live without being the director, that I didn't need the position to be fulfilled." A whooshing sound escaped her lips.

"Wow."

"I know. Wow. I still want to be involved with the board, but being pulled in three professional directions when I'm only one person ... and I don't want my work life to dominate everything else. You have goals too, and so does Ethan. We need to be fully there for each other, and there's only so much of any of us to go around." She took a deep breath, then released it. "Do you think Derek will understand?"

"If he doesn't, you have an answer, don't you? And until you do, I wouldn't make any phone calls to anyone about the Center. Let's see how the Lord plays this out because I have a feeling he's the one calling the shots here."

Something of Ethan's enthusiasm about eating Thanksgiving dinner at Plimoth Plantation entered her own spirit as she packed for the trip on Tuesday night. *Even Craig Reldan won't be spending his holiday with Pilgrim reenactors, or appearing on a nationally broadcast PBS show.* She, Paul, Ethan, and Audrey were going to fly to Boston early Wednesday morning, with Louise and Tim coming from Florida to Logan International where Derek arranged for someone to take them to the Mandarin Oriental Hotel. A studio car would arrive for Erin at two o'clock for the interview.

In addition, her spirit had shed a few pounds when she and Derek reached an understanding about future appearances. She agreed to step in for him while Helen worked to regain her health, but just once a month unless something truly pressing came up, and she would consult directly with his publicist on the details.

Next, Erin told Connie she was turning the reins of the Kichline Center completely over to her, pending Connie's and the board's approval. Her friend had cried then laughed with Erin, making the latter promise she would stay on the board.

Paul wandered into the room and started rummaging in his underwear and sock drawers in his version of packing. They smiled at each other. "I'm so glad everything is working out," she said. "Thanks for your advice."

"My pleasure! I'm happy you've reached positive resolutions."

She closed and zippered her suitcase. "I'm finished here, so I'm going to take a break and read a little more of Grandfather Peter's journal. I haven't had a chance for a couple of days."

Erin climbed onto the bed and pulled the leather volume from her nightstand along with her laptop, opening to where she'd left off.

October 25, 1781

We have won the war. Now we must win the peace.

CHAPTER FOURTEEN

Though his head was bowed in prayer before the beginning of Sunday worship, Peter's attention wandered at the sound of murmuring just behind him and to the left. His trained law enforcement ears told him something had to have happened to unsettle the usual Sabbath tranquility. As he looked up, he saw Catherine's questioning gaze from the corner of his right eye and turned to his left to find the source of the disruption. Hans and Maria Schmidt were entering the pew they normally occupied, followed by none other than Greta Hough and her brood, dressed worthy of a reception with King George himself. Members of the congregation exchanged covert looks and discretely pointed fingers at the highbrow appearance of this new woman in town. He could just imagine their thoughts: "Who is that fancy lady, and why is she sitting with the Schmidts?"

Elizabeth's eyes popped as she leaned over the pew. "Mama, look at the pretty lady!"

Catherine shushed her and gently pushed the girl back into place.

Peter closed his eyes, wincing. He didn't know Greta had arrived yet and certainly had not anticipated such a grand entrance. He'd been planning to visit her father's farm tomorrow to check on her status, yet here she was, settling in with her extended family, wearing clothes that seemed to own her, and her signature startled expression. For a moment, he was back in his house in the early dawn nearly thirty years ago, watching his Margaretta teach young, motherless Greta how to cook and sew, and wondering why she always appeared so worried. Now he sighed to himself. *Oh Greta, you have made a most unfortunate mistake. Instead of blending in, you have called undue attention to yourself, exactly what I had hoped to avoid.*

Following the service, Peter and Catherine greeted several parishioners on their way outside where, at the far right of the entry, Hans Schmidt stood next to his daughter in full grin. A small crowd twittered around them. Peter observed Greta curtsying and offering her bashful smile underneath a bright red hat with towering plumes. Her oldest two sons dutifully shook hands with the curious, but the little girl clung to her mother's skirts, averting her head. She reminded Peter of her mother when Greta first came to Easton.

Pastor Rodenheimer broke away from a talkative man who was providing an extended description of a multitude of disorders and strode over to Peter. Lowering his voice, he spoke out of the side of his mouth. "This must be Mrs. Hough."

"Yes, and her children."

"They certainly are a fine-looking family."

Peter detected a deeper meaning behind the comment. "I didn't know they had arrived in Easton nor had I expected to see them in church this morning. Come, and I'll introduce you." He turned to his wife, chatting with Mrs. Spangenberg. "Excuse me, ladies. Catherine, if you're not too engaged, I'd like you to meet someone."

"Yes, of course." She patted her friend's arm. "I will talk to you sometime this week."

They walked over to the Schmidt party and waited until Michael Gress and his wife had finished making her acquaintance, Peter taking note of Mrs. Gress's raised chin and downturned eyes.

"Well then, I am very pleased to meet you, Mrs. Hough," Gress was saying. "Good day. Oh, hello, Colonel Kichline! Mrs. Kichline." He bowed from the waist. "It's such a fine day for November, isn't it? Everything seems brighter since the war ended."

"Yes, indeed." As they departed, Peter's eyes met Greta's, and he smiled at the look of tender recognition on her face.

She extended her hands. "Herr Kich, uh, Colonel Kichline. How well you are now looking!"

"My dear Mrs. Hough." He took the small hands and bowed. "How very good to see you in far more pleasant circumstances."

"Please meet my children." She spoke slowly, in heavily accented English. Pointing to the oldest, "This is Stephen, then Matthew, and little Eva."

The boys shook Peter's hand, but the girl burrowed further into her mother's side, face hidden.

"Allow me to introduce you to my wife, and to Pastor Rodenheimer. Mrs. Hough, this is Mrs. Kichline."

"I am so happy to meet you," Catherine said.

Normally his wife was among the best dressed women in the village, but Peter observed a marked contrast between her and his former servant. No doubt Major Hough's family had great means, likely supplementing his officer's pay handsomely to have given Greta access to New York's cosmopolitan couturiers.

"I am happy to meet you, too, and you, Pastor. Thank you for all of your help to me."

"It was my pleasure. Welcome to Easton."

"And this is my youngest daughter, Elizabeth," Peter said.

The child curtsied. "Good day."

"Hello, Elizabeth." Turning to Peter, Greta said, "I am eager to hear of all your family."

Susannah Kichline Schneider came over just then, narrowing her eyes, then breaking into a slow smile. "Oh my! Is this Greta Schmidt?"

The woman's gaze darted from her face to Peter's.

"It is you, isn't it?" Susannah gave a laugh. "Oh, do please excuse my poor manners! You are Mrs. Hough. How are you? I am so happy to see you back in the village."

"I, uh, I am not sure who ..."

"Oh, forgive me. I'm Susannah Kichline, the Colonel's daughter."

"Susannah?" The eyes widened. "You were as young as my daughter when I married and left."

"The years have certainly flown. This is my husband, Peter Schneider. Peter, this lady was our indentured servant when I was a little girl."

If Susannah were still a child, Peter would have put a merciful end to her unwelcome chatter.

"I am pleased to meet you." Schneider's face was one large question mark.

"Where is your husband?" Susannah asked, looking around.

"I, I, um, I ..."

Peter could no longer keep silence. "Susannah, perhaps you and Peter would like to join us for the midday meal." He turned to Greta. "You and your family are welcome to join us."

He ignored a disconcerted look from his wife.

"Thank you, but my stepmother has prepared quite a feast, and we must get to it. Colonel, please come to visit us. Soon."

"Yes, Mrs. Hough. I will be out tomorrow morning."

Greta's eyes darted from one curious face to another without making eye contact. "Thank you, Colonel. Papa, I think we'd better go."

"*Ja, meine Tochter. Guten Tag, Herr Kichline, Frau Kichline!*"

Peter watched them pile into Hans Schmidt's comically small carriage.

Susannah spoke up, this time more reflectively. "I have a feeling I may have said something wrong."

"I'll explain over lunch." Peter didn't want to tell Greta's story before the entire village.

Just before they took their leave of the minister, Peter noticed Frau Eckert standing on the church steps, gazing in their direction, arms crossed.

"You jist make yourselves comf'able and, I'll be gettin' dinner," Bett said while removing her cape and hat after church. "Is it all right if William be joining us?"

"Of course," Peter said. He would be smiling right about now had it not been for the disquieting scenes they'd just left behind. "He is always welcome at our table."

"Thank you, Colonel. C'mon, Joe and little Elizabeth. You can set de table."

Susannah piped up. "Do you need my help?"

"No, ma'am. I have plenty."

Peter, Catherine, Susannah, and her husband hung their outer garments on pegs in the foyer then moved into the parlor before the fire which Peter began stoking.

Catherine gave voice to her own thoughts. "What was she thinking, coming to church dressed so dramatically?"

Satisfied with the fire, he settled into his chair and began setting up his pipe, enjoying the warmth after the walk through a village suddenly gone cold. "I think she dressed herself and her children according to the New York circles she lived among."

"I am about to burst here," Susannah said. "What is going on? Why is Greta in Easton, and where is her husband?"

"The truth is, we don't know what has become of Major Hough, and Greta had a sudden decision to make." He explained the nature of her dilemma and how she had chosen to return to Easton. "I had hoped she would make a gradual reentrance in Easton, but she has unintentionally called unfortunate attention to herself."

Susannah picked up the train of her father's thoughts. "Are you concerned there might be some sort of trouble because she is married to a British officer?"

Her darkhaired husband gave a low whistle. "I could see how that might happen."

Peter's mind went back to the way Eastonians had treated Lewis Gordon as a leper after he'd renounced his association with the Committee of Safety and refused to sign the Oath of Allegiance. There'd been quieter cases in which, after making their Tory sentiments known, a handful of villagers decided not to endure public acrimony and left Easton altogether.

Catherine was speaking. "By showing up at all, her presence made people curious, but having dressed ostentatiously, she will be the object of much conversation and curiosity. Why would such a fine lady be associating with the Schmidts? That sort of thing."

"Do you think anyone recognized her?" Susannah asked.

He thought for a moment. "You did. I can't be sure about anyone else." He could still picture Frau Eckert's inquiring gaze after church and wondered if she might guess at Greta's identity. "There are still people here who attended her wedding, although many others, like the Casper Dolls, have moved into the townships." His heart sank. "Those who would remember Greta would also recall she'd married a British officer." He smiled. "For such a timid person, she has always had a way of causing a sensation."

No doubt her father's cozy but crowded farmhouse represented a large step down from Greta's New York residence, one Peter had not seen but could visualize. Sitting in the Schmidts' cramped parlor, he had the sensation of being about to thrust himself into the waves of a heaving ocean. He looked at his wife, grateful for Catherine's feminine support at such a time.

Hans sat next to his daughter, the rays of his smile lending further cheer to the firelit room, a hunting dog reposing on Hans's feet. His wife and young granddaughter busied themselves in the kitchen, having served mugs of hot cider, cups of tea, and molasses cookies to their guests. Peter wondered whether Maria Schmidt was keeping the child busy so the adults could speak more openly. He'd seen the boys outside, doing farm chores, allowing their father and grandfather the luxury of a mid-morning visit with his important guests.

Catherine bought Peter some time, no doubt aware of his penchant of driving straight to a point. They had spoken on the carriage ride along the Bushkill Creek of there needing to be some niceties before he said what needed to be said.

"My dear Mrs. Hough, I do so admire your beautiful dresses, first at church and now this morning. You have magnificent taste."

Greta swallowed a sip of tea and placed the cup on the saucer. "*Danke*. Uh, thank you. I also admire your dress today."

Catherine smiled at her. "My husband provides well for our family."

That was subtle.

"Yes, my husband as well. And his family in England."

Just as I thought.

"Are you very close to them? I can imagine the difficulty of getting to know your in-laws across so many miles of ocean."

"We write each other letters," she said, gazing at the fire. "That is, my husband wrote most of them as I am not educated. They have always been kind to us, to my children, but I do not feel close to them the way I am with *meine Vater*." She looked up at Hans, exchanging a tender smile with him.

"Are they aware of your current situation, Mrs. Hough?"

Sadness sketched the woman's features. "I have not had opportunity, but I must let them know of their son—and our situation."

Catherine lowered her voice. "My dear, what do you know of his whereabouts?"

"Very little." She spread her hands. "He went to the south with his regiment many months ago. At first I heard from him at least weekly, but then ..." Her voice caught. "There were no more letters. I didn't know what to do. I could get no information." A tear escaped, and she swiped at it with a lace edged handkerchief. Her voice became a whisper.

"I had to decide quickly where to go, and I wanted to be with my family in case … my husband never returns."

Catherine leaned forward. "I am happy you have come home."

"I am as well," Hans said. "We will take *gut* care of her and the *Kindern*."

"Yes, I am too, but I told no one where we were going, so they will not know where to deliver any news. That is hardest to bear."

"Your family, friends, and Our Lord are with you in this hardship," Catherine said. "I will help you write to the major's family."

"*Danke. Vielen dank.*"

Ever practical, Peter wondered whether or not Hough's family would continue to provide for his wife and children once they realized he was missing, and she had left the British circle of influence. He couldn't bring himself to ask.

"Mrs. Hough, I wonder if I may suggest something."

Might Catherine be going to mention Greta's wardrobe?

"Yes, of course."

"Your life has changed very quickly," Catherine said. "When you do go into town, I wonder, and please forgive me if I am overstepping, do you and your children have any clothes in keeping more with life in Easton than New York?"

Peter's senses heightened. He could never have been so direct about this sensitive subject, yet his wife had masterfully spoken in such a way as to not hurt or offend.

Greta's eyes opened wider, as if she were

beginning to understand her faux pas at church. "I, I do not. I fear I may have looked ridiculous then, at church?"

"You looked lovely, my dear, just lovely. But you see, we aren't very fancy here."

Hans looked from Catherine, to Peter, to his daughter. "I think Mrs. Kichline may be right, Greta."

"I would be happy to help you arrange a new wardrobe."

Peter sucked in his breath at Catherine's boldness.

"I cannot sew."

"Oh, but I can, and our Susannah is gifted with a needle, as is our servant Bett. We can help you secure material as well."

"I would like that." She smoothed her brocade skirt.

"I think our villagers will relate to you better if you dress more as they do."

"Yes. I understand."

"Very good. Would you like to accompany me to Hart's store sometime this week?"

"*Herr* Hart still has a store here?"

"Yes."

"I remember it well. I would like that very much."

"You may borrow one of my dresses until we get yours made. We're roughly the same size."

"Thank you. You are so kind."

Peter exhaled, as if he'd just sprinted from his house to the river.

CHAPTER FIFTEEN

"Would you look at this!" Erin peered closer at her screen, knowing Paul was in the shower and couldn't hear her exclamation, but unable to hold back. What a perfect day this had been, and now the sight of her grandfather Peter's script, in English. Why he'd abruptly shifted from German to English she couldn't know, but leafing carefully ahead, she discovered what she'd missed earlier—the rest of the journal, with a few exceptions, was written in his adopted language. *This is wonderful! I'll be able to read this much faster now.* While the water was still running in the bathroom, she'd try to come back down to earth from the towering heights of her television appearance by picking up where she'd left off.

November 20, 1781

> Colonel Levers paid me an unexpected, though not surprising, visit today, telling me he had met Catherine and Greta at Hart's store yesterday. Catherine had told me herself she had seen RL, and she introduced Greta as a friend of our family. In the absence of further details, he came to extract from me what my wife would not say about the refined woman

who sat in church with a farmer's family. I told him she and her father had been indentured to me for several years long before his arrival in Easton.

Erin sniggered. *That served old Levers right. He deserved that backhanded dig.* An image of Levers bearing the face of Craig Reldan appeared on the screen of her imagination.

He wondered at the obvious elevation of her worldly circumstances and the whereabouts of her husband. I unfolded her story to him because I prefer he heard it from me instead of piecemeal rumors on the street and in the publick houses. He frowned a good deal, said he was deeply concerned about Greta's capacity for disrupting our community. I assured him her husband is out of the picture at this time, and Greta harbors no political leanings or ambitions. She only has a mind for keeping her family together to the best of her abilities. She has always been a rather simple creature, but I am not certain he was convinced. I have not given thought before this as to what will happen should Major Hough return. If he does, we would indeed be facing an entirely different scenario.

I believe it is time to move forward.

Erin stared without seeing across the room to a modern sculpture on the wall. Had Hough ever come back from the war? If so, did he go to Easton to find Greta or maybe send for her, wherever he was? She didn't think they could easily fit into the village's life after he had commanded forces against the Americans. Although she didn't particularly admire Robert Levers, she did think he had a valid point about the awkwardness of a former British officer taking up residence among a village filled with patriots, still mourning those who'd died and been wounded in the war.

Paul appeared in the doorway to the room wrapped in a towel, his tousled dark blond hair lending a boyish appearance. She caught her breath, still getting used to the fact of him in her life.

"You appear to be deep in thought."

"I was just reading more of Grandfather Peter's diary, which I am happy to report he is now writing in English."

"How nice! You don't have to slog through translations then." He leaned against the door jamb rubbing his hair with the towel. "And what does Grandfather Peter have to say?"

"He's writing about Greta Hough's arrival in Easton, and how Robert Levers came to the house to 'inquire' about her." She sniffed. "It was more like an inquisition. I'd always read about how he had his hand in all of Easton's business, and while I admire his considerable service, he really was a character."

Paul raised an eyebrow. "Something like our Craig Reldan?"

"Exactly." She paused, leaning into the plush bed pillows. "I guess people don't really change all that much, do they?"

"Circumstances and times do, but I think people are people wherever and whenever they come from." He shifted the subject. "You were marvelous on that show today. I'm so proud of you."

"Thanks. When the camera started rolling, I couldn't stop quivering. Even my teeth were chattering." She frowned. "Could you tell?"

"Not a bit. You were fun, charming, and knew your stuff. I think you did Derek proud. You certainly made your family and me proud."

"I appreciate that. Did I tell you he texted me?"

"What did he say?"

"That I was fun, charming, knew my stuff, and did him proud."

He laughed as he walked over and kissed the top of her head. "And just think, now I have you all to myself, just the two of us in a swanky hotel room in Boston, with our parents and Ethan way down the hall."

Her cheeks warming, she laid the book on the nightstand.

"Thanks for calling me, Erin. I'm guessing you're pretty busy after your big weekend."

She went into the family room and sat on the couch, warmed by the soothing sound of her best friend's voice. "No busier than usual, Melissa. And never too busy for you."

"You were wonderful on that show! Tim and I were just so impressed with the way you handled yourself and how much you knew about all those patriots we'd never heard of."

"Thanks. I was super scared at first, but then I calmed down. I think Ethan and our parents enjoyed seeing the TV studio, and we all had a blast at Plimoth Plantation. I felt as if we'd gone right back to 1621 to the first Thanksgiving."

"How magical that must've been!"

"The experience more than made up for the last-minute disruption to our holiday plans. So, what was your Thanksgiving like?" She twirled a piece of hair around her forefinger.

"Quiet, nice. We went to church in the morning for the breakfast—where we saw Al and Pat, by the way. Your father-in-law is looking much better since his surgery. Then I made dinner, and we watched football. On Black Friday, I did some Christmas shopping. It was a madhouse at the Montgomery Mall, but I plowed through and think I'm finished."

"Good for you! I need to do my shopping in earnest now the appearance is behind me, but my book writing is pretty much under control. The deadline is mid-February, and I've been getting up an hour before everyone else to write, then I go right back after Ethan leaves for school."

"Remind me—what's the book about?"

"The title is *Unsung Women of the American Revolution*."

"I'm eager to read it."

"I'm enjoying the research and the writing. Since I don't have all those other responsibilities, teaching and overseeing the Kichline Center, I feel more relaxed with the pace I've been keeping."

"That is a big improvement. Um, about the Center ... are you okay with how everything turned out?"

"More than okay."

"I sense there's a 'but' somewhere."

Melissa had a way of sometimes knowing Erin better than she knew herself.

She lowered her voice. "I'm fine with the outcome, but getting there was painful."

"I understand. That Greg guy was such a stinker."

She didn't bother to correct Melissa. "Yes, well, that's behind me, and now I get to think about Christmas. Since this is our first one as a new family, I want everything to be like one of those sentimental Hallmark movies." She pictured herself surrounded by family, Ethan and Paul, her mom, Paul's parents, who had taken a strong liking to her son, Allen, his wife and girls, and their children, laughing, talking, eating good food, and opening presents around the perfect tree. She made a mental note to ask Alana and Kate what was on their children's wish lists.

"Do you watch those?"

"Watch what?"

"Hallmark Christmas movies. I have to admit, I binge watched a bunch of them when I came back from shopping on Black Friday, then into Saturday. It was like eating a trayful of candy apples. Do you like them with the red or the caramel coating?"

A tangent came roaring down the pike. "Caramel."

"I used to like the red kind until one day when I was at a carnival as a kid, I must've eaten too much popcorn or too much fried dough, and then I had one of those red candy apples and barfed all over my brother on the Ferris wheel. I haven't had one since."

Erin laughed out loud. "Oh, how nasty!"

"You can say that again. I think the carnival was at St. Dennis's. They always had one when I was growing up, and they always had those cheesy prizes at games I swear were rigged. I remember one time ..."

She let Melissa go on a bit while she reached for a pad of paper and a pen and mentally reviewed her gift list, what she'd already bought and what she still needed to purchase. Erin couldn't wait to see her mother's face when she opened her present—her DAR insignia pins. She was more excited about that present than any she might receive herself. She also needed to decide what baking she would be doing, and whether or not they'd be having Christmas at her place, or Allen's. Funny, she thought, she hadn't heard from him in a while. In the midst of her lightheartedness, she had a sudden, wrenching realization she wouldn't be buying a gift for her dad this year.

"So, are you?"

"Um, am I what?" she asked through a thick throat.

"Excited about Christmas?"

"Oh, yes, I am."

"I do want to get together. Maybe we could have lunch? Or is your schedule too tight?"

"I could definitely meet you for lunch." Her mood began to lighten again.

While Melissa mentioned a few possible dates, Erin suddenly burst into hysterics.

"What in the world?"

"Oh, Melissa!" She gasped for breath. "You should see this!" She started laughing from deep in her stomach. "Toby just trotted into the room covered in toilet paper!"

"Well, for heaven's sake, get off the phone, take a picture of him, and text it to me!"

Erin did as she was told.

She called the older of her two nieces the following day, eager to discuss their Christmas plans. After initial chitchat about their kids' activities and the weather, she dove in head first. "I'm wondering if you'd like to get together the Sunday before Christmas, or right afterward."

A harbinger of silence iced the room.

"Aunt Erin, we won't be in town. We're doing Christmas a little differently this year."

"Oh?"

"We decided to take a family vacation."

She injected artificial lightness into her response. "Where are you going?"

"Disneyworld."

"I went there for Thanksgiving last year, and we had a good time."

"Yes, I remember."

"I guess I'll see what Kate and your dad are up to then."

"Um, they're going to Disney too."

Erin squeezed her eyes shut, her vision of a new and brighter family experience collapsing. Didn't they realize this was their first Christmas without their grandfather, or that this was Erin and Paul's first Christmas together? Alana's words,

"It's a family vacation," repeated. Clearly, Erin, Ethan, and Paul weren't part of that family. She spoke around a desert-dry throat. "When will we exchange gifts?"

"I don't know. Maybe we can get together after the new year."

Her spirit rose to meet the challenge, like a child who decides to take her ball and go home. "We'll see."

Before they hung up, Erin found courage to say something she knew needed to be said. "Alana, I hope you have a nice trip, but realize this is going to be very disappointing for your grandmother. She loves Christmas, and for her it looks a certain way. I think you, your sister, or your dad need to let her know your plans, the sooner the better."

"Oh, okay, Aunt Erin. I'll give her a call."

There was no way she was going to step into that minefield, even if she would be the one cleaning up the shrapnel.

When she told Paul about the conversation, Erin read the disappointment in his face as well. "I have a notion not to buy them any gifts at all." She was in full sulk. Why did people have to ruin things for others?

"I can understand that, but I wouldn't cut them off entirely. Maybe just mail them some gift cards for their trip."

She pursed her lips. "Yes, I could do that," she said. "I just hope they don't forget to give Ethan presents."

He squeezed her hand, and she experienced the soothing of its warmth and familiar roughness. "I have an idea. Let's go get a tree!"

She'd missed most of Easton's post-Thanksgiving revelry, the lighting of the Peace Candle in Centre Square, and the Bachmann Players' appearance singing colonial carols at Scott Park when the mayor lit the Christmas tree. She'd originally planned to share these hometown heart warmers with her new in-laws, but they'd had other joys in Boston and Plymouth. Erin now sat in her usual pew at church next to Paul and Ethan on the second Sunday of Advent, warmed by the sanctuary's seasonal transformation. As the organ played "Jesu, Joy of Man's Desiring," she scanned the bulletin announcements. There was, fortunately, still time to purchase memorial poinsettias. She'd want to participate to honor her dad and her grandparents. She also expected to see something about the work of the historian who'd been combing through the church's ancient documents, and who'd discovered Grandfather Peter's journal. She knew he was supposed to have completed the job about now. She hadn't seen him around church, and Paul had been too busy with work and family to keep up with the project.

Following the service, Erin wandered up to Pastor Stan in Fellowship Hall, the din of dozens of conversations covering her as she waited while he finished talking to the head elder in a guarded tone. She saw Ethan with his Sunday School teacher, and she'd left Paul with a visiting family in the history room off the main hall. When the elder had the last word with the minister and turned away, she stepped forward.

"Ah, Erin, how good to see you this morning!" Stan Grube grinned. "I thought you were wonderful on that show. You seemed as if you'd been doing television all your life."

"Thank you, Pastor Stan. I had a lot of fun." Something about the minister struck her as distracted, the way he kept looking in other directions.

"Were you very nervous?" He took a sip from his paper coffee cup.

"Terribly, but I knew many prayers were being said for me, and God helped me calm down."

He tipped his head, seeming to try and focus on her. "Do you think you'll be doing much of this in the future?"

"Possibly. Derek McCutcheon won't be able to make appearances for a while, and we're working on a manageable schedule for me to substitute."

"I'm sure you'll continue to do very well, Erin. I'm happy for your success."

"Thank you." She fingered the scarf around her neck. "Uh, I'm wondering something. I thought by now the historian the church hired might be giving a report or presentation."

Stan coughed into his closed hand. He motioned for her to follow him to a quieter spot near the back of the hall where he told her, "I'm afraid we just lost our funding for the project."

"Oh." Her eyes clouded as she swam through her thoughts. "What happened?"

"The grant money, well ..." He turned away as if to prevent himself from saying more than he should.

Erin's skin prickled. "Who provided the grant?"

"Craig Reldan's foundation."

CHAPTER SIXTEEN

Stepping out of his bed chamber straight into the path of two cyclones in the shape of a little girl and a bigger boy, he flattened himself against the wall to avoid impact.

"Make haste Joe or we're going to be late for school."

The lanky adolescent tripped over his feet, stuffing his shirt into his breeches. "I'm coming, little Lizzie. I'm coming!" He skidded to a stop, apparently more concerned with not being rude. "Good morning to you, Herr sir Colonel!"

Peter laughed. "Good morning to you, Mr. Joe."

The boy grinned as he and Elizabeth thundered down the steps toward the dining room where Bett was placing a platter of hoecakes and scrapple on the table and waited by their chairs, bodies vibrating with energy while Catherine poured herself a cup of coffee, and Peter made his way to the head. Elizabeth and Joe scraped their chairs against the floor and flopped into them once he was seated and watched for his cue to pray.

"Good morning, wife," he said, caressing Catherine with a tender look. "Will Jacob be joining us this morning?"

"He was up before de roosters," Bett said, hovering over him.

Peter savored the moment, his youngest living son's industriousness, the shining faces of his small daughter and Joe, Catherine's steady beauty of face and spirit, Bett's warm ministrations and friendship. He invited his family to join him in prayer.

As soon as he uttered "amen," the children pounced on their food quite forgetting their table manners, scarfing down pancakes and meat. Peter sipped his hot, black coffee, watching them over the rim of the cup while they washed down the hasty meal with goblets of milk.

"Papa, may we be excused?" Elizabeth passed her napkin across her mouth.

"What's the hurry?" He looked at the mantel clock and realized they were not late at all.

"Mr. Spangenberg said if we came to school early, he would teach us to make eggs."

He moved his head forward, lapsing into German. "*Entschuldigung*?"

Elizabeth turned to Catherine, her expression pinched. "Oh, Mama, would you please explain this to Papa? We really musn't be late."

"Yes, of course dear. Remember your mittens. There was a heavy frost again last night."

Bett had disappeared and returned with a small basket. "And here be your eggs. Y'all don't want to be forgettin' them."

Joe snatched the container, and for a few minutes, the cyclone wheeled and spun again through the house then out the front door with a resounding thwack.

Peter chortled. When he'd been a prisoner of war, he had often called to mind such domestic scenes, cherishing them in his heart. He found even his children's most irksome behavior a continual source of charm, and he frequently reminded himself not to fall into a ditch of indulgence. He swallowed a moist forkful of hoecake and turned to his wife. "Tell me, what is this about eggs? Is our Mr. Spangenberg now teaching them how to cook?"

Catherine's eyes glimmered. "No, my silly husband. He's going to show them how to decorate eggs for our Christmas tree."

"Ah, of course." He smiled. "I hope they were empty eggs, or he'll surely have a mess on his hands."

"Indeed they were. Bett and I used them for gingerbread and *stollen* yesterday."

Stollen. Dense, fruity, powder-dusted. His favorite Christmas dessert. He leaned back, licking a drop of maple syrup off his bottom lip before speaking. "I remember my mother reserving the eggs she'd used for Christmas baking, then helping us children decorate them for the tree. My clumsy hands shattered more than I created." He gazed into the distant memory. "My brothers always had a more delicate touch." Coming back to the moment, he pursed his lips then asked, "Isn't it a bit early to be decorating eggs and baking for Christmas?"

She shot him a tolerant look. "Christmas less than two weeks away. We are just getting started."

"I'm glad you came this morning, Papa," Jacob said. "I'd like to talk to you about something." He headed toward the entrance where he stationed himself.

Peter preferred to go outside where they couldn't be overheard, but a snapping wind and bone-deep cold caused him to reconsider. Instead they put their heads together and spoke in undertones, him reading uneasiness in Jacob's pinched expression. The matter he had brought to discuss would have to wait. "What is on your mind, Jacob? Are you all right?"

"I am fine." He shifted from one foot to the other.

When the cat seemed to get the young man's tongue, Peter pressed gently to ease out what must be difficult words. "What has happened?"

"It's Stephen Hough. He, well, he is, uh. . ."

"Is he not working out here?" Peter looked toward the back of the mill where the boy was loading processed grain into sacks, his shoulders as hunched as if he were personally carrying the weight of them.

"He has learned his job quickly, and he is the last to leave at the end of the day. I have no complaints about him, however, others have expressed their displeasure by taking their business elsewhere."

Peter scowled, crossing his arms over his chest. "What happened?"

"Frau Eckert came here a week ago and asked in a rather strident manner"—he lifted his chin and adopted a high-pitched voice—"'Is it true you are employing a traitor?' She did this right in front of Stephen. I would never strike a woman, Papa, but

I had to restrain myself. And her breath just about flattened me!"

His throat ached. "Frau Eckert's behavior was reprehensible."

"There have been several others." Jacob informed his father about other long-term customers who were taking their business to Bethlehem, despite the inconvenience.

His teeth grinding, heat flushed through Peter. How dare those people misjudge his decision to hire the son of a woman who most probably had lost her husband and her home in the war! He didn't need his pipe; he was smoking.

"Papa?"

He closed his eyes, then faced his son. "I'm listening."

"What should we do?"

He knew what he wanted to do—gather the miscreants and thrust them into the stocks for a long afternoon in the biting cold. Teach them a lesson. This, however, was not the Christian response and, in fact, reduced him to their level. Wisdom and grace must be brought forth, but he could not naturally manufacture them. He needed to think. To pray.

"Don't do anything for the time being, son." He gripped Jacob's shoulder. "Just carry on. We'll figure something out."

As he left the mill, Peter looked in Stephen Hough's direction and when their eyes met, he offered the lad a closed-lip smile.

"Of course I will pray with you, Colonel." Pastor Rodenheimer leaned forward in his chair, sitting with his friend before a glowing fire in the minister's parlor. "This is a difficult situation indeed."

"Understand, I am primarily thinking of the Hough family, not my finances."

"I never thought otherwise."

Peter sighed. "Angry as I am, I do begin to understand those who are boycotting my mill. The war has been so long and bitter, and the people of Easton lost so many. Making peace with one's opponent comes with time, and so little has passed."

"You are right, of course. If we respond to the losses with anger and revenge, we are acting out of our fleshly nature, but we must instead look to our Creator, who restores the years the locusts eat, and makes all things new."

He looked into his pastor's eyes. "I need to connect with that source of power and grace to meet this challenge."

"Don't we all?"

Elizabeth and Joe bounded into the house with the same energy they'd taken with them to school. He wished he could somehow tap into their vitality. He willed himself to pleasantness, laying aside his newspaper as they greeted him, getting as near the fire as they dared.

"So, where are the eggs you decorated today?" he asked.

"Oh, Papa, something this important takes time." She planted a kiss on his cheek with her chilled lips.

Out of the mouths of babes. She's exactly right. This situation is going to take time. Patience and time. Grace and time.

They were just finishing the evening meal when William entered, having let himself in through the back door. Bett rose from the table, beginning to gather empty plates and used silver wear. "If y'all will excuse me," she said.

"Of course. I imagine your friend will be hungry." Catherine winked at the woman, who blushed.

Elizabeth piped up. "William is her sweetheart, not her friend, Mama."

Peter reached over and mussed his daughter's hair. "You must not speak brashly to your mother."

"I'm sorry, Papa."

"Tell her not me."

"I'm sorry, Mama."

"I quite accept your apology," Catherine said. "Now then, help Bett."

Elizabeth and Joe hopped up and started collecting serving dishes and glassware.

"Would you like some coffee, Colonel, Miz Kichline?" Bett asked.

"Yes, I would, thank you," he said.

"I would as well. Would you like a hand?" asked Catherine.

"No, ma'am. You just go and relax. You bin at it all the day long."

They moved into the parlor where Peter added kindling to the low-burning fire, then settled into his chair. "Tell me, Catherine, what have you been doing today?"

"The usual." She waved her hand. "Bett and I made and delivered soup to several families, then we went to Mr. Hart's store for some ingredients for our Christmas baking." She sighed, looking into her lap. "Oh, darling, while I was there, Hans Schmidt came, and all of a sudden, the place was colder inside than out."

He straightened his spine. "What do you mean?"

"Customers scowled and turned their backs. I went to him, but he would barely acknowledge me. I think he must've been concerned others might shun me as well. He paid for his items with neither he nor Mr. Hart saying a word, and as he left the store ..." Her voice trailed, then she whispered, "I saw someone—I don't know who it was—spit on him."

Tears streaked down her face, and he reached across the table for her hand. He hadn't told her about the situation at the mill and sincerely doubted Jacob had said anything to her either. He wanted to protect her from further distress.

"I am deeply disappointed in our village's response to Greta and her family," he said after some time. "I expected better of them, although not all."

"I thought there might be some tension but never dreamed there would be such boorishness." She wrung her handkerchief. "There's more, Peter."

He didn't want more. He was up to his very eyeballs with "more," but this was his wife, and she needed his consolation more than he needed to mollycoddle his own spirit. Fortunately, the arrival of Bett with the coffee tray bought him some time.

"Thank you, Bett." Catherine sipped her coffee then clinked the cup onto the saucer with a trembling hand. "You know how Greta bought all that material for new, more appropriate clothing?" He nodded, and she continued. "I found out quite inadvertently she spent most of what little she has on the project."

"I'm not sure I understand fully." He inclined his head to the side.

"Because she left New York secretly, any money the British army might have coming to her because of her husband's service is lost. Nor do her in-laws know where she is just yet, and even when they do, they might not come through for her. Her husband had considerable savings, but she doesn't know where he kept them." She bowed her head. "I feel awful having suggested the new wardrobe, which hasn't done a bit of good anyway in gaining acceptance in this community."

He shouldered the weight of her grief. He had to try to fix this, to do something to clean up the messy situation. "My dear, we can at least make a present of those clothes, saying they were a Christmas or homecoming gift, whatever seems right. You were only trying to be helpful so do not be so hard on yourself." He blew out a sigh. "As for the future, another solution will need to be found. Hans already has his large family to support."

"Thank you, dearest husband. You show me such grace." She paused, seeming in search of some semblance of hope. "Thankfully, Stephen is working at the mill now and can bring in some money."

When William appeared in the doorway, clearing his throat, Peter nearly jumped out of his chair and embraced the man for bringing a most welcome interruption.

"Pardon me, Colonel. Does this be a bad time for you and the Mrs.?"

He rose and beckoned William into the parlor, shaking his hand, watching the fellow's mouth fall open. "Come in, come in. We welcome your presence. Please, have a seat." He waved toward the chair reserved for his guests as he resumed his sitting position.

"I don't mind standing, sir."

"I wouldn't dream of it. Will you have coffee?"

"No, no, thank you." His eyes darted from Peter to Catherine, then back. "I can come another time."

"Not at all, William. We were just relaxing after dinner. Please do sit."

"Thank you, ma'am." His right leg jiggled and when Peter's eye wandered there, William suddenly stopped, rubbing the back of his neck instead. "I wanted to come by tonight to talk about something, um, something important."

Peter closed his eyes against what he fully expected to be another sad chapter from the Schmidt family saga. "Is something troubling you, William?"

The dark eyes opened wider. "Uh, no sir, not at all. I am not troubled in the least."

The tension in his middle slowly eased. "This is good to know, but I detect something is on your mind."

"Yes, yes, there is." William looked up from an inspection of his hands. "I want to tell, uh, ask you and Mrs. Kichline, something."

"We're all ears," she said.

"Well, I, uh, I … you see, there's something I'd like to do, and I think it only proper if I get your permission."

Peter pressed his lips together wondering what William was getting at. He was, after all, a free man who could do whatever he pleased. "I am prepared to give a blessing, son, but you hardly need my permission for anything."

"Begging your pardon, Colonel, I think in this case I may need both." He ran a finger under his collar. "You see, a father is gen'rally who a man goes to, but there is no father."

His head prickled. He knew where this was going.

"I would like to marry Bett, and it's only fitting I ask you for her hand."

Catherine leaped from her chair, squealing and clapping her hands together. For a moment, she and Elizabeth seemed to have exchanged places. "Oh, how wonderful!" Then she paused and looked at Peter.

He broke into a grin. "This is excellent news. I think the two of you will be very happy together if, of course, she agrees."

"I think she will. I've been hinting enough, but I didn't feel right asking outright without talking to you first since she belongs to you."

"Bett belongs to herself." In case he'd come across too gruffly, he asked, "Where will you plan to live?"

"I've been saving toward buying a property where I can set up my woodworking shop and live on the premises."

"Where is it?"

"The house of Conrad Fartenius."

Peter hadn't known his deceased private's wife was planning to sell. His face tightened, very much disliking to be told what everyone else seemed to know.

Catherine spoke. "I heard she was planning to remarry."

"Remarry?"

"Christina told me her intended is a soldier who briefly served on Colonel Levers's staff. He'll be returning to Easton for good in a few days, and they are to be married just after the Sunday service on December twenty-third."

"How very nice for her," he said. "Will they be staying in the area?"

"He bought a farm in Williams Township."

He gazed at her, marveling how she seemed to know everything.

William stood there wringing his hands, seeming to wait for an end to the discourse about Conrad Fartenius's family. "Uh, Colonel Kichline, there's something else I'd like to ask you."

"Yes, of course, William."

"Well, you see, if Bett will agree to have me, I would like to bring Joe to live with us."

The breath caught in Peter's throat. Take Joe, the boy he loved as a son, the little fellow who once shadowed their late housekeeper Frau Hamster wherever she went, and who addressed him with manifold titles all at once? The boy who was showing deep creative promise? He sensed Catherine staring at him and caught her glance, reading in her eyes sadness and understanding. The idea was not preposterous. "Why do you want to do that, William?" He thought he already knew but wanted to hear the words spoken.

"He has been a little brother to me since those bad days—before you took us in. I know he's happy here, and if you want to keep him, I understand. I would just like the three of us to be our own family."

"Does Bett know what you're thinking?"

"She knows I'd like to have Joe with me when I buy my business."

"I see." Stalling, he took a deep draught of his cooling coffee. "You would keep him in school, would you not?"

He flung out his arms. "Oh, yes, I would, Colonel. No doubt about the boy being educated."

"What about Bett?" Catherine asked. "Would you want her to continue to work?"

He wasn't sure the way his breath kept stopping and starting were good for his heart.

"As long as she wants."

Though relieved, Peter realized she might choose a different path if she accepted William. That was entirely her decision. They would manage in any case. He slapped his palms against his thighs. "Well, then, when do you think you'll speak to Bett?"

He broke into a grin. "This very night."

CHAPTER SEVENTEEN

She lowered her reading glasses and the chaotic Christmas list to admire the heartwarming tree and the candles Paul had placed in the windows, wondering if she'd made the right decision about the ornaments they'd elected to use. Somehow displaying the ones she and Jim had collected over the course of their twenty-year marriage had struck a dissonant note in her spirit. She wouldn't dream of tossing them, and she didn't want to deprive Ethan of his memories of Christmases past. This was his second one without his father, his first with his stepfather. She still thought Paul's solution the most soothing—have two trees, one for the living room featuring new ornaments and a second for Ethan to design that would go in the family room. Her son would choose any decorations he'd grown up with and add any he might want to add. Her one disappointment was how Ethan had demonstrated little enthusiasm at the store, spending most of his time shrugging his shoulders and saying things like "Sure" and "I don't really care." To be fair, Erin thought, the boy totally disliked shopping.

She stroked Toby's head as he lay at his usual spot by her feet then studied the few remaining items on the scattershot, heavily marked gift list. Ethan hadn't picked out a present for Paul. She wondered if the opposite were also true. Paul had said he was going to take Ethan to buy her gift, but had he been able to pull it off? Every time Erin suggested to her son they go downtown to choose something for Paul, Ethan had an excuse in the form of a headache, stomachache, or homework. She really didn't want to pick out a gift on her own for her son to give his new stepfather. She wanted this to be the perfect kind of heart gesture, something to cement their bond. A sudden thought popped into her mind: "These things can't be forced. They take time." Erin huffed. The two of them got along well and enjoyed each other's company. She thanked God Ethan hadn't developed any kind of nightmarish attitude toward Paul as seen on TV, yet when it came to this gift-giving thing, her son dragged his heels. She went cold at the thought of giving her son the option not to buy a present for Paul, imaging the pain her new husband might experience if Ethan didn't. Was receiving a lame gift any better, though, one presented totally out of obligation? *Lord, please help me know what to do. I'm at a loss here, and I want this first Christmas with Paul to be perfect for all of us.*

They'd just picked up a pound of chocolates at the Easton Public Market for Ethan to give his grandmother when Erin sensed an opportunity. The chatty clerk had asked him what kind of chocolate he liked best, and upon hearing "the peanut butter kind," had given Ethan a handmade "Reese's"-type candy, gratis.

"Thank you. This is really good," he said around the mouthful.

Erin couldn't help but notice the lighter step, the shining eyes. "That was nice of her," she said. "You know, Ethan, Paul really likes when the vendor who sells gourmet vinegar in the next kiosk gives him samples. That might make a nice present for him, from you."

He wrinkled his nose. "Really, Mom, *vinegar?* I can do better than that."

Her heart gave a small leap, and she held herself back from sounding overly eager. "I'm sure you could. What were you thinking?"

"Well ... You know those books they have across the street?'

"Do you mean at the Sigal Museum Store?"

"Uh-huh. He likes history, so I thought maybe we, uh, I could get him one."

"I'm sure he'd love that." She paused as they walked toward the main entrance, swathed by piped-in Christmas music and the deli and seafood vendor's pungent aromas. "Was coming up with something to give Paul hard for you?" She hoped she'd sounded casual.

"Yeah, sort of. I mean, I always knew what Dad liked, so that was easy."

All at once she remembered how, on every gift-giving holiday, he presented Jim with some kind of new tool.

"I'm still getting to know Paul."

Her eyes shone, locking on her son. There was no resentment here of any kind, just a kid navigating a new situation. "Well, I think you know him better than you may think."

"How?"

"You know how much he loves books."

"Yeah, he's always reading. I even thought of getting him one of those electronic readers."

This was amazing. Ethan hadn't been dragging his feet; he'd been trying to figure out where to step. "You did?"

"Yeah, but he doesn't seem to be the e-book type. He likes to hold the old-school kind."

She gave a laugh. "You're right about that."

As they emerged from the Sigal Museum laden with multiple bags, both of them having completed the last of their Christmas purchases in the winsome shop, Erin saw Connie walking toward her from the direction of the Kichline Center. She frowned at the drawn expression on her pert friend's face, and as she drew nearer, Connie showed no sign of having noticed Erin or Ethan. Not until she was within arm's length did she look up, and stiffen.

"Oh, hello, Erin. Hi, Ethan."

"Hi, Mrs. Pierce! We've just finished our Christmas shopping."

"How nice for you."

Erin cocked her head to the right, narrowing her eyes. "Hi, Connie. Are you all right? You seem ill."

"I, uh, yes, I'm fine."

"Hey, Mom, I think I want to buy another one of those chocolate bars with the Easton Bugler on the wrapper. Is that okay?"

Grateful for the opportunity to talk to Connie alone, she fished in her bag for a five-dollar bill. "Here you go."

"Thanks! I'll be right back." He took off across the street, having looked both ways first, leaving his mom and her friend on the sidewalk.

She wouldn't beat around any bushes. "What's wrong, Connie?"

Her eyes darted from left to right, and she pulled Erin away from the Sigal Museum's front entrance, toward Bank Street. "This must be kept strictly confidential, Erin. I need someone to confide in, and you're just the person."

"Of course. I won't tell a soul, not even Paul if you'd rather I didn't."

"Not just yet. He'll know soon enough." She took a deep breath and didn't speak again until a couple passed beyond their hearing. "I got a call from the bank this morning that the check I wrote for the head contractor bounced. I couldn't figure it out because our second installment from the Reldan Foundation came in two weeks ago." Her chin quivered. "When I dug deeper, I discovered the money had never reached the bank. I called the foundation office and got an automated message saying the number had been disconnected."

Erin's heart thudded, immediately recalling what Pastor Stan had told her about the church historian's grant not coming through. She asked with a husky voice, "What's going on?"

"I can only guess, and I'm not sure what to do." She wrung her leather gloved hands. "I had to get out of the office for some fresh air. The walls felt like they were closing in."

"Is anyone else aware of this?" Her eyes followed Easton's mayor greeting two women across the street before entering Public Market.

"Only you."

She was thinking on the fly. "I guess you could call an emergency board meeting or maybe contact Herman Weinreich and see if he knows anything."

Connie appeared lost in a maze of thought. Then, "I like the idea of going to Herman since he's the Center's Lafayette connection." She reached out and pressed Erin's arm. "Will you go with me? I mean, do you have time?"

Erin saw Ethan emerge from the Public Market and signaled to him. "Yes, of course. Ethan can hang out in the history department lounge while we talk."

They found the history professor in the hall closing the door of his unruly digs. His eyes flashed question marks. "Well, hello. To what do I owe this pleasure?"

"We need to talk to you," Connie said.

He pushed the door back open and turned on the light, moving to clear two chairs bulging with academic rubble so they could sit. "If you had come any later, you would have missed me. I just corrected the last of the finals for the semester." He sat back down, unzipped his jacket, and crossed his arms. "So, what is on your minds?"

Connie spilled the contents of her story and when she finished, Herman stood and wandered to the window, seemingly observing the bare trees swaying outside. Then he thumped back into his chair, grimacing. "I haven't seen Craig for a few weeks, and he gave no indication of anything being wrong. This may just be small hitch."

Erin went ahead and told him about the church historian's failed grant, watching as Herman ran his right hand through what was left of his hair.

"I must tell you ladies, this news has left me quite at a loss for what to say. The situation certainly bears closer scrutiny, and I will start looking into the matter."

They parted, telling each other "Happy Hanukah," "Merry Christmas." The perfunctory wishes were the best they could do.

Paul had gone out front humming and smiling to fetch the paper and place a bill in the mailbox, but returned appearing dazed.

"What's wrong? Your face is so white." Erin's stomach rolled.

"Look at this." He showed her the front page.

Her hand flew to her mouth. "Oh my! Oh wow." She stared at the headline.

Craig Reldan Arrested.

"What in the world!"

He sat down, began reading aloud. "'Late Sunday

night local entrepreneur and philanthropist Craig C. Reldan surrendered to local authorities and is being held in the Northampton County Prison pending bail. Last week his wife, Anya Reldan, filed for divorce citing her husband's alleged criminal activity. Investigators have discovered he had been funneling money from his eponymous foundation into his personal bank accounts. Further inquiries revealed the foundation had not made payments to several grant recipients during the last two fiscal quarters, while those receiving checks could not cash them.'"

When Paul finished, Erin exclaimed, "Serves him right for all damage he's caused!"

He remained close-lipped, broody. Annoyed, she wished he would say something, agree with her, craving his validation while something inside scolded her. Yes, Craig was a stuck up, arrogant, horrible person, and what he had done to her, and now many others, was very wrong. But hadn't God said something about not gloating when your enemy faced ruin? She'd have to look that up.

Paul had gone to his office, and Erin returned to her laptop to pick up the threads of her writing only to confront a mental block roughly the size of the Free Bridge. Her creativity had collapsed under the weight of Craig Reldan's implosion. His wife was divorcing him. He'd been caught stealing from his foundation. He was currently in prison awaiting bail. He'd reneged on commitments to the church, Kichline Center, community college, and at least a dozen other Northampton County nonprofits whose buildings might end up going dark, with employees laid off and recipients of their services denied. At Christmas. How many children would go without presents or celebrations or families without adequate food or heat? She pictured Craig in his monogrammed shirt, sleeves rolled to the elbows, sitting on the side of a lumpy prison cot, head in his hands. A vein pulsed in her temple. At least her mother hadn't called her demanding to know what on earth was going on. Apparently, her Aunt Fran, who subscribed to the paper and shared whatever she considered worthy of repeating with Audrey, hadn't broken the news to her yet. Erin didn't feel like talking to her mom about the debacle just now, needing time to process the scandal, and her response.

Sighing, she saved the two paragraphs she'd managed to write across as many hours and closed the document, opting for a two-mile walk with her dog in the biting cold, working off her shock and anger. Back home in the warmth of her kitchen, Erin prepared a cup of hot tea and slathered a red velvet cupcake with tartar sauce, then returned to her office. She needed to connect with her grandfather Peter's age-old wisdom, with his story. She settled into her chair, Toby snuffling against her sock feet, and opened the link to his journal.

December 19, 1781, Easton, Penna.
My good wife and household are thick into Christmas preparations. Even Bett, who

was raised in the South, has embraced the German customs. She is especially fascinated with the figure of Belsnickel and is in as much anticipation and dread of his sudden appearance as Elizabeth. These days, however, her face is especially radiant with the prospect of marrying her William at the start of the new year. He is preparing a home for them where Conrad Fartenius once dwelt with his family. Pastor Rodenheimer will perform the ceremony on the first day of the New Year.

Erin smiled at the thought of his housekeeper's upcoming marriage to the man whose name had come up before and wondered what their personal stories were, how they had come to know her ancestor and be part of his larger family. Since Bett was Southern, what had brought her to Easton? And what about this Belsnickel, a figure she'd only heard of once or twice in passing? She thought he might be a kind of anti-Santa, who went around punishing kids who made the naughty list. She continued reading.

Were that everyone in the village shared the joy of the season and the prospect of marriage. An ill wind blows in the general direction of Greta Hough's family. Her son Stephen came to Jacob and Andrew just yesterday, offering to quit working at the mills. Because we have employed him, and his father was, or may be, a British officer, several customers have rather vocally removed and taken their business to Bethlehem. I strongly urged my sons to keep Stephen as a matter of principle. I am hoping my fellow citizens will repent of their sinfulness in favor of taking care of orphans and widows in their distress—should Greta be a widow.

Likewise, Robert Traill informed me of an

unfortunate incident in which Hans Schmidt discovered excrement smeared on his front door, and one side of his best horse whitewashed. Greta is in such distress she will not leave the house, mourning not only her husband, but what she regards as the evil she has brought upon her father's household. Hans and Maria stand firm, as I am, in our belief the storm will pass.

Erin pinched her lips together, huffing imaginary steam from her ears. Why were people being so vindictive? This woman was trying to keep her family together in a place she was very fond of. She hadn't fired guns or cannons at Continental soldiers, and she chose to live with people who stood on the opposite side as her husband and his family. Shouldn't she have had a chance for a fresh start? Furthermore, what would happen—what had happened all those years ago—if, and when, Major Hough returned from the war? If he tried to live in Easton, what feathers that would have ruffled! She shook her head, uncertain how she herself might have responded to Greta's family, knowing one thing for sure—she wouldn't have whitewashed anyone's horse or smeared poop on a front door.

At times I almost despair at the depths of depravity in our human nature. I am reminded that unredeemed men can inflict the vilest of offenses against their Creator and His creation. To these painful realities, however, speaks the fact of Christmas. While we were yet sinners, Christ came to live among us, and to die that our brokenness might be put right.

The truth took her breath away.

CHAPTER EIGHTEEN

Peter found John Spangenberg in the one-room schoolhouse clearing the detritus of a day's teaching, so intent he didn't see his former commander until he bumped into him and looked up.

"Oh my! Hello, Colonel!" He laughed, clutching the broom to his burly chest. "Obviously I was deep into my thoughts."

"And your task." He enjoyed laughing with his friend. "I do apologize for startling you. May I say, you are as handy with that broom as any *hausfrau*."

He grinned. "I am a stickler for neatness."

"Which made you an excellent quartermaster."

Spangenberg bowed his head in acknowledgment. "You are most kind."

"And the schoolhouse looks quite festive." He took in the Christmas decorations the children had made, dangling from the ceiling, filling the deep windowsills.

"Like any good German, I love the holiday. Yes, the ornaments have turned out nicely. I must say, your Joe is showing signs of being quite the artist."

"I have suspected as much."

"Let me show you his work."

Spangenberg led Peter to a window toward the middle of the classroom and pointed to one of the hanging egg shell ornaments, standing out with its plethora of expertly applied dashes of gold and red. Peter leaned in for a closer examination and noticed the boy had embedded a tiny nativity scene of intricate detail.

"His work is most impressive."

"Yes, Colonel. The inspiration comes from a deep well."

Peter considered how, in just a few weeks' time, Joe would be leaving his household to live with Bett and William and asked the teacher if he knew about the arrangement.

Spangenberg scratched his balding head. "I did not. He will stay in school, yes?"

"Absolutely."

"I think you will miss his presence in your home, but what a fortunate young man to have lived with you and now to be with a new family."

"He and William have a long history together."

The teacher moved his head back and looped his thumbs through his waistcoat. "So I have heard." He paused. "You seem to have something on your mind, Colonel."

He released a deep breath. "Yes."

"Won't you have a seat then?" Spangenberg motioned toward a chair opposite his own at the front of the room, swathed by the soft glow of candlelight against the gathering gloom of a deep December twilight.

Peter looked into his friend's eyes. "Can you tell me how the Hough children are getting along here?"

The teacher made a tsking sound as he rubbed the back of his neck. "They are nice children, well-mannered, and have maintained high marks in their schoolwork."

"But?"

"They keep to themselves, speak only when spoken to, not only with me but with the other students."

"Have any of the children caused them distress?"

He frowned as if he understood the colonel's hidden meaning. "I wish I could tell you otherwise, but there have been two incidents of taunting, and one in which the Esser boy was about to launch a fist at Matthew Hough."

Esser. Peter recalled the gruff manner of Easton's first butcher, a man known for his volatile temper, a regular before Northampton County's Quarter Session courts. *This must be his grandson. The apple doesn't fall far from the tree.*

"I imagine you have intervened then."

Spangenberg looked him in the eye. "Every time. I do not believe the sins of the father should always be visited upon his family." He stopped for a moment, gazing toward the floor. "I know what it is like to be treated unjustly."

Peter recalled the painful episode just after the Battle of Brooklyn in which both his son, Peter Jr., and Spangenberg had been brought up on what turned out to be false charges of cowardice. "I thought you would respond as you have, but I needed to hear you say the words. Thank you for standing up for this family, my friend. They are, as you can imagine, in a difficult situation."

"As I understand you are as well?" He cocked his head.

"What?"

"Word has spread about some who are boycotting your mills because you employ Stephen Hough."

He closed his eyes, not wishing to discuss this.

"We are not promised that doing the right things will be easy." Spangenberg cleared his throat. "If I am not mistaken, didn't Mrs. Hough and her husband provide aid to our imprisoned Flying Camp?"

"You are not mistaken."

"All the more reason for coming to their aide. Is the husband lost then?"

Peter scratched his left temple. "His whereabouts are unknown. Major Hough is a man of integrity who would not deny his family under any circumstances. If he is not dead, then he is disabled somewhere."

"And if he is alive and returns to Easton to rejoin them, they will face another set of problems and decisions." He stared past Peter, silent, the wind tapping at the windows. "I must share with you a most touching story, Colonel. Earlier this week the little Hough girl struggled with her egg decorating In fact, she broke three shells and was on the verge of tears. I was about to assist her when Maria Fartenius got up from her desk and slid next to Eva. I heard her ask whether she could show Eva how to handle an egg so it wouldn't break. The child told her she had used all the eggs she'd brought, and Maria gave Eva the last one she had."

Peter's eyes moistened, a Bible verse coming to mind: "And a little child shall lead them."

He passed by Bett's room on his way downstairs and heard the ladies of the house twittering. Curious, he paused by the half-closed door and inclined his head toward the joy-filled clatter, trying to shrink himself from their view, no easy feat for a broad-shouldered man of six feet-two.

"You're so beautiful, Bett!" Elizabeth was exclaiming. "Mama, isn't she be-yoo-tee-ful?"

Catherine's chiming laughter gave way to words. "Yes, darling, she certainly is."

He guessed his housekeeper was trying on her wedding togs, a household undertaking second only to Christmas preparations. Recently Catherine had immersed herself not only in baking and garlanding the house, but finding a suitable bridal dress for Bett, as well as planning a reception at the Green Tree Inn after the church ceremony.

He moved past the door congratulating himself on his elusiveness then shot off the floor when Catherine called out to him.

"Oh, darling, you must see Bett's wedding dress!"

"I, uh, I ..."

"As if we didn't see you lurking around the door." She clearly enjoyed seeing Peter squirm, a sight not often seen. "Not to worry. Come in." She waved him inside.

He caught his breath. Was this Bett—this stunning woman standing before him, a queen with her two attendants? The only times he ever saw her dressed up were at church, then she'd hurry back home and into her workaday apparel. Now she was a visual feast of bridal loveliness, a certain pattern in the fabric catching and reflecting the candlelight on her radiant visage. Peter stood there gaping, then recovered his dignity. "Bett, you are indeed a beautiful young woman. I can only imagine how happy and proud William will be when he sees you in that dress."

"Thank you, Colonel." She gave a curtsy. "You and Miz Kichline are so very good to me, making me a present of this dress. I never had such finery, almost feel guilty for it."

Peter stepped close to Bett and wrapped an arm around her shoulders. "Every woman should be at her finest on her wedding day."

He could see from the strain on Greta's face she was trying to produce mirth worthy of the evening, but she frequently lapsed into sullenness, shrinking into her chair as if to make herself disappear. The startled look had returned. He and Catherine had invited the Schmidt family for dinner the Friday before Christmas, and Peter had grown weary of the whole affair. Catherine, who rarely committed such an offense, chattered mindlessly, but her efforts to engage their guests were as thwarted as the Easton ferry in a rough current. Even the children at the overflow tables, sat morosely moving their forks from their plates to their mouths. He glimpsed the mantle clock, wondering how much longer he could stand this.

He and his wife jumped up, the others gasped and yelped at the sound of a loud thwack on the window. Silverware clattered against plates and onto the floor.

"What in the world?"

"Oh my goodness!"

"What was that?"

Hans's and Maria's four-year-old girl reared back her head and howled, and her mother gathered the child into protective arms.

Peter turned to the window behind him, Elizabeth and Joe signaling in its direction, the other children in various states of alarm and excitement, crying out "Look! Look!" He rose and drew closer, breaking into a smile. "I do believe Old Belsnickel has come to see the children!"

Catherine pressed a palm to her heart. "Of course! Belsnickel."

The Hough children were frowning.

"What is Belsnickel?" Stephen asked, putting his arm around his little sister's trembling shoulders.

"Why, young man, he comes to visit children just before Christmas to determine who has been naughty," Peter said.

Matthew Hough's eyes were as startled as his mother's. "Wh-what d-does he d-do?"

He bent down and smiled. "In our household, very little. Only good children live here, right Mrs. Kichline?"

Catherine appeared relieved to no longer trying to be the sole source of entertainment this evening. "The colonel is correct. Belsnickel will find no trouble here, and he may even have a treat for each of you."

The alarming figure had withdrawn from the window and could be heard pounding on the front door. The children squealed and danced in place as Peter went to answer the summons. When he opened the door, he looked past the strange costume into eyes he immediately recognized, those of Peter, Jr., a man with the heart of a child, who as yet had no children of his own. Peter gave him a wink and said with a loud voice, "Come in, Belsnickel! Welcome to my home." He waved the figure inside, the children gathering in the hallway, huddled against one another, a mass of quivering excitement.

"That's an animal!" Eva Hough cried.

"I am no animal, young lady," bellowed the tall, bearded figure. Clad in head-to-toe fur, he carried a birch switch in one hand and a small sack in the other. "I have come to find any naughty children living in Easton."

Peter's sensitive nose wrinkled. The fairy tale creature smelled very much like a wet dog.

"There's none here." Elizabeth inched closer, reaching out to touch the thick fur. "I like your coat, Belsnickel."

The scary being patted her head. "And I like you, Elizabeth."

Her eyes flew open wider. "You know my name!"

"I know every child's name." He proceeded to match each little one to his or her moniker, right down to the Houghs.

"I've been good this year," Joe said.

"And what have you done that was so good?"

"I help Bett around the house and study hard."

Elizabeth was not to be outdone. "I started reading, and I pray every night before I go to sleep."

"So I have heard." He reached into the sack and produced a piece of candy in the shape of a cane. "You shall each have a reward."

All the children except Stephen, who appeared to cling to his oldest child dignity, surrounded Belsnickel, cataloging their good deeds. Except for the littlest one who tugged at the creature's arm. "I was a bad girl yesterday."

Belsnickel crouched to hear Eva's confession. "What did you do child?"

"I sassed my mama yesterday, but I am sorry."

"Did you tell her?"

"Uh-huh."

"Did you tell God?"

"Uh-huh."

"And you will not sass her again?"

"No, Mr. Belsnickel." She squirmed. "I will try not to."

Each of them received candy. "Now then, children, you have been good this year, but you must take your obedience and kindness into next year, and I will see you again."

With a flourish, he left as theatrically as he'd arrived, leaving behind a transformed dinner party. Peter prayed there would be more, and better, reasons in the days ahead for the Houghs and Schmidts to find repose for their weary souls.

Normally the church emptied at the end of Sunday services, each going to their own homes for a large repast with family and friends. Not so on the twenty-third when Christina Fartentius invited everyone to stay afterwards to witness her nuptials to Captain Levi Newton. The sanctuary swelled with members of Robert Levers's military staff, impressively turned out in their handsome, though somewhat threadbare, uniforms as they rejoiced with their comrade in arms. Following the ceremony, the party rambled on a fresh inch of snow to the Bachmann Publick House for a reception enlivened by an energetic fiddler and a vast array of meats, breads, pickled vegetables, and cakes. The festivities kindled a warm glow in Peter, an exclamation mark after Mrs. Fartenius's harsh season of loss. William and Bett sidled next to him wearing broad grins.

"Well, then," he said, "are you contemplating your own wedding?"

Bett blushed as her intended's smile stretched across his attractive face. "Oh yes, sir."

"If my wife has her way, your merriment will surpass even this."

"She is so very good to us," Bett said.

Peter gazed into the earnest brown eyes. "You are part of our family."

Bett squeezed her eyes shut but not before a single tear escaped.

The couple disappeared into the vibrant crowd toward the back room of the first floor. He guessed over half the village had turned out, but of course, not the Hans Schmidt family, who had not gone to church this morning. Before he could gnaw on that subject again, Peter saw the bridegroom making his way toward him, surprised to be singled out. More than a few hands slapped him on the back as he passed by.

"Congratulations to you, Captain."

"Thank you, Colonel." He bowed from the waist. "My new wife has made me the happiest of men."

"She is a fine woman, and her daughter is as lovely as her mother."

"Indeed, I know this to be true." His eyes darted past the fireplace. "I wonder if I might have a private word, sir."

"Of course."

"I do believe there's a quiet spot over there."

He followed Newton beyond the bar where Robert Levers held forth and the hearth where some of Peter's family huddled near the fire.

"I have been most eager to share some of my story with you, Colonel, if you don't mind, as I believe our stories somewhat overlap."

"Certainly."

"You see, I spent the early part of the war on General Washington's staff in New York."

"I see."

"I'm aware you led the Northampton County Flying Camp at Long Island."

"Yes."

"That was a bad business, so many fine men lost, including my wife's first husband." He pressed his lips together.

"He was a gallant fellow. In every way, he fought the good fight."

"Indeed. I believe I should have enjoyed knowing such a man and feel honored to be able to take care of his family." After a short rest he continued. "The General thought highly of you and your men. He often spoke of your bravery to others, how by holding off the British and Hessians as long as you did, you made the escape of his remaining troops possible."

Peter couldn't push a response past his lips.

Seeming to understand, Newton continued. "I got around New York quite a bit in those days, but few people knew I was affiliated with the General." He gazed meaningfully at Peter.

He cocked his head. "Were you a spy, then?"

He responded with a barely discernable movement of his head. "I posed as a merchant and did all I could to procure supplies for our troops who had such a bad time in and around New York. In my work, I encountered a British couple who often aided my efforts to provide relief for the imprisoned American troops. To be exact, the husband was a British officer, the wife, a German."

His skin prickled, the laughter and music receding.

"Once they realized what I was doing, despite the danger to themselves, this couple often provided not only food and clothing, but money. I knew very little about them, as they preferred to remain anonymous, but when the husband was sent away from New York, his wife on several occasions related information she received from him and her other British sources about troop movements. Once when I told her I would be leaving for an assignment here in Easton, she told me she had lived here a long time ago. She said her former employer had been imprisoned by the British, and she tried to help him and his remaining men."

"Greta," he mouthed, standing stock still. "Greta Hough."

"Was that her name?"

His throat gathered wool, turned his voice hoarse. "Yes."

"I have often wondered exactly who she was and what happened to her and her family. I don't suppose you might have a clue?"

Peter emerged from his state of shock. "Her name is Greta Schmidt Hough, and I sponsored her and her father's journey to America in the early 1760s. Shortly after my first wife died, Greta met and married a British captain, and not long after that, he was stationed in Philadelphia. Her father established a farm on some of my outlying property and married a Leni Lenape woman."

"Do you happen to know what has become of Mrs. Hough? I often think of her courage, her commitment to our Cause."

Peter closed his eyes. "Oh, yes, indeed I do."

He spread his hands. "I would very much like to meet her, if at all possible."

He answered with a grin.

CHAPTER NINETEEN

She contemplated the tablet on her nightstand wishing she had a block of time to sit in her easy chair and pick up where she'd left off in her ancestor's diary, eager for a resolution to Greta Hough's predicament. On this Saturday before Christmas, however, with Ethan and Paul watching cartoons downstairs and a bakery's worth of cookies ahead, rooms to clean, and a few more presents to wrap, she smoothed the bedcovers and adjusted four decorative pillows before turning off the light. In the hallway closet, she gathered the dusting wand and some furniture polish and marched as if to war to clean the guest room, followed by the family library. Paul's parents would be arriving on the twenty-third to stay four nights, and Audrey would spend the twenty-fourth bunking on the library's sleeper sofa. She'd also been able to talk Pat and Al Miles into coming up for dinner on Christmas Day.

When she finished dusting, polishing, and vacuuming, Erin went downstairs to her office, fired up her desktop computer, and headed straight to her inbox. She quickly marked spam emails about the miracle uses of apple cider vinegar and tape strong enough to lift a Mack Truck. She opened one from the DAR State Librarian, a confirmation letter about her appearance at the April state conference for the book club, and answered in the affirmative.

She spoke aloud. "Here are more invitations." Hatfield College was asking if she'd come and speak at a consortium for writers, and a producer at WFMZ in Allentown was inviting her to be interviewed on air about her book with Derek McCutcheon. Her own star definitely seemed to be rising, and she could almost hear her dad saying, "I'm so proud of you," his brown eyes gleaming. She hadn't known his approval earlier in life and had never tired of his affirmation in the season before he died. She wiped at a tear as she glanced at a photo of him in his Army uniform.

Back to the inbox. Urgent messages followed from the George Taylor Chapter and her church's volunteer coordinator, sounding a great need; because the Craig Reldan Foundation wouldn't be providing gifts for the Children's Home or a community meal for the homeless and disadvantaged, gaps needed to be filled. As the regent, Connie Pierce implored the ladies to host a Christmas Day dinner at the community center, and First Church had the names of local children from the Home and various agencies who'd been counting on the foundation to supply gifts.

Erin wanted to help, happy to supply food for the Christmas Day dinner, but with her family visiting and a meal at her home already planned and purchased, she couldn't commit to being a server. Buying gifts would mean a shopping trip and as she considered the meager days remaining until Christmas and her tight schedule, she sighed. The only time she could get out would be tomorrow, the Saturday before Christmas when all the procrastinators came out of the woodwork ready to mow down anyone in their path to acquire a last-minute wide screen TV or at-home pedicure boxed set. *Maybe I could buy the items online!*

She shot an email to the church's coordinator asking for the names of five children and their wish lists, hoping for a prompt response. By the time she had gone through her inbox, Sandy Haggerty had answered, providing information for three girls and two boys, including their sizes and preferred colors. Erin went straight to work online only to admit defeat an hour later when there were no guarantees the items could be delivered on time.

If she never heard "Rockin' Around the Christmas Tree" again ... She'd been at the Walmart long enough to hear their holiday music loop twice, plus she'd heard the same song in the car on the way to the store and once again while circling the congested parking lot like a vulture waiting for a spot to open. Just as she was about to occupy the one she'd waited for a while, a family loaded the contents of a bulging cart into their minivan, taking their time turning on the engine and pulling out. Erin simmered when a Mini Cooper bolted from the other side to claim the prize. She finally secured a place and, gathering her bag and keys, joined the frenzied throng with the kind of dread she reserved for her annual gynecology exam. Paul had offered to go with her, but she insisted he stay home with Ethan and tackle her recipe for Toll House cookies figuring—how hard could that be? Of course, she knew what the kitchen would look like when she returned. Every sheet pan and dirty mixing bowl would litter the countertops, and flour would have spilled onto the floor she'd just mopped, with the ingredients for the cookies left out for her to put back.

An hour and a half after the commencement of her shopping expedition, she stood fourteenth in a line with a cashier who moved at the rate of a sleep deprived sloth, and the guy in front of Erin suffered from a nasty case of flatulence. She'd tried to use the self-checkout, but that line snaked all the way back to the produce department. If her cashier took ten minutes to process each bloated cart, Erin realized she might be caught in this purgatory for two more hours. This was definitely not how she'd planned to spend this Saturday when she'd awakened with an idyllic image of festive cooking shows in the background as she filled her spotless kitchen with Christmas aromas, then wandered into the family room with mugs of tea and chocolate chip cookies to play Risk with her guys.

If not for Craig Reldan, she wouldn't be in this mess. Her attitude nosedived. Her father wasn't here to celebrate the holidays with her and her new husband. Her brother and his kids had ditched a family Christmas in favor of the Mouse.

At least Craig won't be having a good Christmas. Released from jail two days earlier, he'd gone back to his million-dollar, gated community home to find his wife had fled with their children to Palm Beach, Florida. *He deserves it.*

She had barely pulled into the garage when the inside door opened, and Paul and Ethan stood ready to help her schlepp bags into the house, Toby hot on their heels.

"Well, hello! This is nice to come home to," she said, slipping out of the driver's seat.

"You sounded pretty stressed in your texts from the checkout line." Paul bent over to kiss her.

"I hope you two are ready to wrap presents."

"We are!" Ethan said.

She hugged him sideways. "You're the best."

"No, you're the best."

She grabbed four of the lighter bags and stepped inside where she tried to find a surface they hadn't littered. She sniffed at a charred aroma clinging to the air. This day just kept getting better and better.

Ethan staggered in under the weight of a half dozen plastic bags. "Look, Mom! We made those cookies." He pointed to a cooling rack next to the sink where they'd stacked their creations. "Try one!"

"Okay, okay, just let me get out of my coat and put my purse down." Her son hopped from one foot to the next while Paul brought the remaining parcels into the house and, finding no more room in the kitchen, let some of the contents spill into the family room.

"Did you leave anything for the other shoppers?" he asked, eyes twinkling.

"Just barely."

He came over and hugged her. "You did a very good deed, and I'm proud of you."

"Thanks. For a while there I was feeling as if no good deed goes unpunished."

Ethan followed her back to the counter and stood there grinning at the Pisa-like display. "Go ahead, Mom!"

She reached for one of the cookies, noting the scorched underside. "Oh, uh, this one looks a tad over-done."

"Those were the first ones. Then Paul turned the temperature down. These are better."

She followed his gesture and chose one from further back. Only half of the bottom had been so afflicted. She bit into the cookie and savored the melting bittersweet chocolate, followed by a nasty jolt of rock-hard char.

"How do you like it?"

She looked into her son's eager face and knew she couldn't tell him exactly what she thought. "The chocolate melted perfectly."

"I'll bet Nana will love them!"

She smiled at him as she finished off the rest of the cookie, swallowing several times to keep her gag reflex in check. Then she noticed a large box perched against a side wall. "What's in there?"

Paul shrugged his shoulders. "I don't know. The UPS guy made a delivery about an hour ago. The label has your name on it and since it's Christmas, I didn't think I should open it."

She hugged him and took his Swiss Army Knife, carefully working her way through heavy packing tape. Paul tipped one end of the container while she slid the contents, covered in glittering gold wrapping paper, toward her. Unwrapping the gift, she discovered a navy blue Bigger Carry-On bag. "This is beautiful!" She began working the latches and opened the suitcase, marveling at its array of compartments.

"I like all those pockets," Ethan said. "Who's it from?" He shoved a cookie into his mouth.

"This card fell out of the box." Paul handed the envelope to her.

A moment later, she smiled. "It's from Derek." She read aloud, "'To Erin from Derek. May you have many happy adventures with this suitcase. Merry Christmas to you and your beautiful family.'"

"That was so nice of him, so thoughtful, and I only sent him a card."

"It's customary for an employer to buy a Christmas gift, or give a bonus, to an employee," Paul said.

"Yes, I suppose so. Still, I wish I'd thought of sending him something."

He winked at her. "There's always time to go back to the store."

She swatted him with a piece of foam packing material.

"Hey, Mom. Paul and I have an idea." Ethan bounced with enviable energy.

All she wanted was to fling herself on the couch and close her eyes. "Um, what's your idea?"

"We want to go down to the Winter Village to ice skate."

"Tonight?"

"Yeah, tonight." His eyes widened in expectation.

Paul intervened. "I think what your mom needs is to lay down for a while with her feet up. She's been doing battle with last-minute shoppers and cranky people in parking lots."

"Oh, sure, of course."

"How about you and I start wrapping all these gifts, then we'll all go down to the Winter Village? Do you think you could go after you rest?" Paul asked. When she hesitated, he added, "You know, Ethan, maybe you and I should go ice skating. She's had a really big day, one she hadn't planned and didn't especially enjoy."

"Oh, right." Ethan's pout said otherwise. "What if we get all the gifts done and clean up the kitchen?"

"We need to do those things anyway. Let's get to it, and we'll see how the rest plays out."

Erin caught her husband's eye and mouthed "Thank you."

She nestled in her bedroom chair with a cup of decaf Christmas blend and opened her tablet. "Well, Toby, what do you think happens next in my grandfather Peter's saga?" The basset hound regarded her with wide eyes, then laid his head back on his paws. Warming to the familiar writing, she picked up where she'd left off.

December 23, 1781
Yesterday Pastor Rodenheimer came to call

bearing a letter from the Rev. Burton in New York. Through his contacts he discovered what has become of Major Hough, and he asked if we might convey the sad news to Greta and her family.

Erin flinched as she read on.

We rode out to the Schmidt farm and found Greta helping her stepmother in the kitchen. When she looked into my eyes, I could tell she knew something was amiss for she asked, "What have you come to tell me?" She sat down straightaway. I might have wished for a better time and place but then is there ever an ideal way to tell someone her husband has died?

"Major Hough died!"

She bore the news quietly, holding up while her family began to gather around her. She held her children close, all but Stephen, who suddenly took on the appearance of the man of the household. Greta wanted to know what had become of the major's body, and I told her he had been buried with his fallen comrades near the place he fell. All the cheer left the farmhouse, and we stayed for two hours. Pastor Rodenheimer promised to do a funeral right after Christmas, and Greta expressed her appreciation but said she did not believe the village would approve. Both he and I assured her there would be a service whether or not anyone at all approved. We would be honoring her husband and the father of her children, not a British soldier. When we at last left, Pastor Rodenheimer said he would see them at church on Christmas Eve, and Greta said she could not. She was not welcome. "I welcome you," he told her. "Indeed, you must come." Then he looked into my eyes, and I knew she must be there, and we must do our part to set things to rights.

She wanted to read more, but as she mulled over the meaning of the last sentences, wondering what Peter had meant, the tablet slipped from her hand, and she succumbed to sleep.

CHAPTER TWENTY

He stood to the side as William and Joe hefted a cut fir tree into the front parlor, looking over his shoulder to make sure Catherine and Bett didn't see the snow clinging to its branches melting onto the floorboards. Fortunately, they were in the kitchen with Elizabeth and his daughter-in-law Sarah turning out gingerbread worthy of his German childhood, the aroma teasing his senses. He needed to turn his mind to something else before he marched right down the hall and snatched up the very dough as he'd done upon entering Easton after being released as a prisoner of war.

"Let me give you a hand setting the tree up, William. Joe, run into the kitchen for some rags or something to dry the floor."

"Yes, sir, Colonel!" The boy only knew one speed, and he went with haste on his new mission.

William frowned as they settled the tree into the wooden base he'd fashioned. "I do apologize for the disorder. I thought we'd shaken the snow all off."

"This is the nicest tree we've had in many years." He stepped back to take in the joyful spirit he always caught with a Christmas tree in his home. "As long as the ladies don't see the puddle, we'll be fine."

Joe returned with his mouth full and a large rag.

"Did anyone ask why you wanted that?" Peter pointed to the boy's right hand.

He displayed sodden ginger bread as he spoke without first swallowing. "Uh-huh, but I told them it's Christmas, and you aren't supposed to ask too many questions."

Peter let go a laugh and watched as Joe bent down to the floor, taking the better part of ten minutes before the tree shed its watery load. In a case of perfect timing, the females descended upon the parlor with trays of stringed popcorn and cranberries, the latter, a special order from Massachusetts that Peter had picked up at Hart's.

"What a lovely tree!" Catherine exclaimed, touching the branches.

"Do you think you could find another one for Lt. Kichline and me?" Sarah asked William.

"I think so, Miz Sarah. We could do that, couldn't we Joe?"

He nodded and smiled.

"I would be so grateful," she said.

"Papa, look! We made garland for the tree!" Elizabeth shoved one of the trays in front of her father, and he bent down to voice his approval. "You'll have to help us string it because you're the tallest person in the room."

Joe thrust his little chest out. "He's the tallest man in all of Easton!"

Peter's heart warmed, remembering how, as a young boy, he used to boast of his late father's prowess. For some reason, his parent occupied the center of his thoughts today. He'd had so few holidays of any kind with Johann Andreas Kichline, but putting up the family tree remained among his most cherished memories, along with joy-filled outbursts upon discovering the *Christ Kind* had left a gift for each family member on Christmas Eve. He smiled to recall how his mother wanted to wait until Christmas Eve to display a tree but, little boy-like, his father insisted they should have it ready at least three days before so they could linger over its stately grandeur.

He brought himself to the present as Elizabeth handed him the first of the popcorn strands. "We'll do these, then the cranberries. However did you find them, Papa?"

Joe spoke up. "He can get anything he wants, can't you, Mr. Colonel?"

"Perhaps not everything, Joe." For one thing, he didn't have Abraham, who'd lived during most of Peter's captivity in New York, and died before he'd had the opportunity to know him. He shook himself free of the sorrow, immersing himself in the festivities, even joining in the singing of "O Tannenbaum," however off-key.

Joe disappeared for a few minutes when Elizabeth brought out her egg shell ornaments from school, along with a dozen more she'd fashioned with her mother and Bett. Peter could easily tell who had made each one, his daughter's with a child-like charm only an affectionate parent could fully appreciate. When the tree appeared to be completed, Joe entered the room carrying a small basket and, with averted eyes, handed the parcel to Peter and Catherine.

"I made this for you, for my Christmas gift, so's you'll never forget me."

Peter's heart clutched. Was Joe regretting the fact of his leaving the household in a little over a week, or just coming to terms with it? He squeezed the slim shoulder. "I, we, could never forget you."

"Ever," Catherine said.

Peter took the basket and reached in to find the Christmas egg he'd so admired at the schoolhouse, remembering how Mr. Spangenberg had spoken of the boy's burgeoning talent. "Joe, this is exquisite." He marveled once again at the tiny figures of the Holy Family, amazed such a young boy could do such intricate work.

"He's the best artist in our school." Elizabeth grinned, revealing a newly-missing front tooth.

"You're not so bad yourself," Joe said.

"Maybe not, but no one is like you."

Peter smiled at her lack of jealously and, thanking Joe, placed the ornament front and center on the tree.

He found Joe sweeping the kitchen for Bett after the day of heavy baking, pleased to find they were alone for once. "You are an industrious and gifted young man."

Joe looked up and grinned. "Thank you, sir, Colonel." He looked down at the floor. "Uh, thank you for everything. If you hadn't come along when William and me were on the block …"

The ugly sight reared up in his memory. "Providence brought us together." He put a hand on the boy's shoulder. "I want to make sure you want to live with Bett and William. You know you are most welcome to stay right here if you would rather." He scolded himself for any undermining his words might cause, not wanting to sway the little fellow one way or the other.

The response seemed to come from a far older person. "I 'ppreciate it, thank you. I feel sad about leaving here, but I think I belong with William and Bett now."

He struggled to understand. "If you ever change your mind, my door is always open, and your room will be available."

Joe did something he never had before. He rushed into Peter's outstretched arms.

"Colonel Kichline, Pastor is here to see you, and he's wit another man."

Peter rose from his chair and his newspaper. "Thank you, Bett. Please show them in." He was about to greet the men when his voice caught at the sight of the minister's solemn expression. His gaze traveled to Rodenheimer's companion and gave a start. "Pastor Burton! You have come a long way, and just before Christmas." He reached out to grasp the man's icy hand.

"I am pleased to see you again, colonel."

"Won't you both have a seat?" He swept his hand to indicate chairs nearest the warming fire then looked from face to face. "May I offer you a warm drink, some cider perhaps, or tea?"

"Nothing, thank you," Rodenheimer said.

Burton closed his eyes as he shook his head "no."

Peter slapped his palms against his thighs. "Well, then, how may I be of assistance?"

The men looked from one to the other, then the minister from New York dove into the deep end. "I have had further news about Major Hough."

"I see." He leaned forward. "What has happened?"

"As we knew, he had gone south to engage General Washington in Virginia, and just before Yorktown, Major Hough was discovered relaying his regiment's battle plans to the Continentals."

He bit the inside of his lip, sensing where this story might be going.

"The British seized him and were about to execute him when the American soldiers who received the message returned with reinforcements, a scuffle ensued, and they managed to rescue him. In the fray, he took a bullet to his leg. He appeared to improve after the first three weeks, and I understand he expressed a desire to return to his home and family."

Peter's stomach clenched.

"Unfortunately, he succumbed to his wound two weeks ago in Delaware. The commander of the American unit tried to get word to Mrs. Hough, and through a series of events, I received the news, then a letter the major wrote to her." He produced an envelope with a seal. "I didn't want to share only partial news when I first sent word of his death."

He closed his eyes. *Stephen Hough was a spy.* "Where is his body?"

"They buried him near Wilmington with some other soldiers."

Rodenheimer spoke. "We are on our way to visit Mrs. Hough and thought you might want to be there when we share the news."

"Yes, yes of course. This will come as a shock to her." He waited a moment to see if there was anything else, and when neither man offered additional information, Peter stood. "Well then, let us be on our way."

Eva Hough buried her face in her mother's bosom as Greta patted her back, her sons solemn. Hans and Maria Schmidt huddled close to them, their own children forming a protective circle.

Peter couldn't find anything worthy to say at such a moment, and in fact, no one spoke for most of the visit. He thought of Job's comforters who, in the earliest stages of that ancient fellow's massive grief, sat silently with him. He was not one to question the Good Book. Before taking his leave, he took and held Greta's hand for a long moment, gazing into her eyes, surprised not to see in them the enduringly startled mien, but peace of the kind which passes understanding.

As midnight approached in the hushed sanctuary, he breathed deeply the scents of melting candlewax, pine boughs, and something like hope itself. He surveyed the glowing, expectant faces of his family and friends, all seemingly on tippy toes to hear afresh the ancient refrain of the angels. The shrouded heaviness of the war years was giving way to a new and glorious morning, infusing meaning into the loss and burdens patriots had born with courage and resolve. He looked in the direction of Robert and Elizabeth Traill, smiling upon his dear friends, then at the proud Levers family, who nodded in response.

Hans Schmidt led his family down the center aisle and stood befuddled to find his usual pew occupied by Frau Eckert, her scowl matching her notorious breath. Her children and the congregants seemed to take a collective, sharp breath. Peter's sunny mood evaporated, replaced by the kind of sourness reserved for pickling. He imagined the thoughts racing through people's minds—"How dare *they* come here?" "Loyalist scoundrels." "Traitors!" But he knew better, and he sat poised, anticipating the serving of justice. Tonight.

Peter stood and waved toward Schmidt, whose eyes widened at the summons, who pointed a finger at his own chest and mouthed "Me?" Peter waved again, and his family started to make room for their scorned friends. "Please join us."

"But ..."

Elizabeth patted the seat next to her. "Sit next to me, Eva."

The little girl gazed at her mother, who whispered, "Go ahead."

Murmuring broke out like a pox, and Peter ignored the acid looks and remarks as he would deflect the very darts of Satan, which he considered to be in the same league. Mercifully, the organ began playing *Geboren Ist Uns Der Heilige Christ*, soothing the savage breasts, at least temporarily.

Peter participated half-heartedly during the prayers and readings, angered how people who made up the Church in Easton could treat a beleaguered family with such venom. Especially tonight. He sat back and crossed his arms when Pastor Rodenheimer entered the raised pulpit to preach.

"We read in the Holy Book of the Christ child bringing peace on earth, goodwill to men, and we claim to be his people, his representatives, yet as I look out tonight on my flock, I see only a few who are living in such a manner. When my heart should be filled with joy over the greatest news ever brought by angels to this weary world, I see far too many ravening wolves in our midst."

A collective gasp filled the church. Peter had never seen his good-natured pastor in such a state.

"Many of us have rejoiced this past fall in the cessation of a war that took a great toll on all of us with no exceptions. We have looked forward to a new season of peace, but I ask you tonight, how can the Christ bring us peace when we are still swinging swords of hatred and haughtiness?" He puffed out his chest and began imitating them. "'I did more to support the Cause than you.' 'I paid more taxes.' 'I fought in more battles.' If we follow along those lines, we will tear each other apart like ravening wolves!" With a resounding smack, he thumped the pulpit with the flat of his right hand. "And let me tell you something else. If you cannot find it in your heart to forgive your supposed enemies, just as Christ forgave those who nailed him to a cross for your sins and mine, he will not forgive you."

He gripped the sides of the pulpit, as if to catch his breath.

Peter glanced sideways at Greta, who sat on the other side of his wife, both of them pop-eyed.

"There is among us a young woman who came here to Easton from Germany as a girl and left as a married woman. She married a British officer in those days well before the Revolution, and both of them were deeply patriotic toward America. Because of their efforts, efforts that put them in great jeopardy in the aftermath of the Battle of Brooklyn, many of our brave and suffering men were given enough food and clothing to make it back here to Easton after their imprisonment." He leaned over the pulpit. "Right up until the end of the war, Major Stephen Hough used his influence as a British officer to advance the Cause of the land and people he had come to love and admire so deeply, and he lost his life because of it." Rodenheimer had emphasized each of the last eight words.

Peter had never before heard such a communal gasp. The once-proud faces of the congregants made way for open-mouthed humiliation, stooped shoulders, concave chests. The flaming arrows of truth had reached their targets. Even Frau Eckert was in tears.

The pastor hadn't finished.

"Tonight, on this holy night of peace and goodwill, when our Lord came to earth to show us a new and better way to live, I call upon my flock to repent and not only receive the good news of the gospel but to exhibit his grace."

Rodenheimer closed his eyes, and the Bible. While he took a seat, the organ struck up "Hark! The Herald Angels Sing."

Peter had never heard the beautiful words sung with such meaning, or accompanied by so many tears.

In the glossy midnight blue, on the snow-covered ground encircling the church, Greta Schmidt Hough and her family received good tidings of great joy, the greetings and love of Eastonians, who had gone into church one way, and who left transformed. He marveled at the sight of Frau Eckert embracing Greta, of the Esser boy shaking Matthew Hough's hand.

Elizabeth Kichline stifled a yawn with her mittened hand, leaning into her father's chest as he held her against him.

"Papa?"

"Yes, *Liebling*."

"What just happened?"

He smiled into her innocent eyes. "Judgment happened."

"Judgment?"

"Yes, followed by repentance."

"Then what?"

"Grace."

"God's grace?"

"Yes."

She seemed to draw from a deep well. "Christmas came tonight."

"Yes. Christmas came tonight."

CHAPTER TWENTY-ONE

She awakened before the alarm to the garbled conversation of her husband and in-laws, a clanging of cookware, the clinking of utensils, the rising scent of coffee. Erin reached for her cell phone on the night table—six-thirty. She hadn't planned to rise until seven and gladly received the gift of a half hour to herself on a day of wall-to-wall interactions. She could reach back into her ancestor's journal to find out what had happened to Greta and her family, to people whose bodies long ago had turned to dust, but whose stories continued to pulse with life and significance.

Sitting up in bed, she opened the diary and clicked on her lamp, hoping for a happy resolution, or at least the beginning of one to Greta's rock and hard place situation. A suggestion of daylight crept just outside the closed blinds as she scrolled to where she'd left off, the entry dated December 26, 1781.

Easton, Penna.
The Christ Kind has left us all a most wonderful Geschenk, for not only a family has been restored to Easton's bosom, but the village

itself is once again clothed and in its right mind.

Her heart gave a leap. She devoured the next words.

> At the Christmas Eve service, Pastor Rodenheimer scolded the congregation up one side of Northampton Street, then down the other for our haughtiness, our weighing each other in the balance of our own scales regarding who was the most patriotic—who had sacrificed sufficiently for the Cause, who was lacking in support. He told us in no uncertain terms enough was enough, and we must rise above our sinfulness. The war is over, and now is the time for grace and healing. We all sat at rapt attention to hear our mild minister speak in such a fashion.

Erin smiled as she pictured the pastor in his flowing robe, eyes blazing, quite literally pounding the church pulpit.

> He spoke of Greta's assisting American prisoners at great personal risk and cost, not only in the aftermath of the New York campaign when my men and I received her life-giving ministrations, but continually thereafter. As eyebrows raised and mouths swung open, he told the story of her husband's death after being exposed at Yorktown of relaying messages to the Continental Army.

Her scalp tingled. *Greta's husband died while spying for our side.* She could imagine the stalwart officer standing before a firing squad, wondering if he had perished in such a fashion. Even as she mourned his tragic end, Erin triumphed in Greta's vindication and, driven to know what else her Grandfather Peter had to say, read on.

> Greta and her family, although in deep mourning, have entered into a better situation here after our good pastor's disclosure and admonition, although her finances remain precarious. Many repented for scorning and persecuting this beleaguered woman. Two men apologized to me for withdrawing their business over my employment of Stephen Hough. I observed a most compelling scene when Frau Eckert welcomed Greta back to Easton.
>
> My soul magnifies the Lord, and my spirit rejoices in God my savior, who has poured out His richest blessings on my family, friends, and Easton, where He once again has been welcomed into our homes during this glad Christmastide. Glory to God in the highest, and peace on earth, goodwill to men.

Erin's tears flowed. There wasn't any more. She had uncovered all the wisdom he had to impart in this journal, yet the story didn't seem to be entirely over. Sitting quietly for several moments, reflecting on the condition of her own soul regarding a certain enemy of Easton, she prayed to have the right attitude. Afterward, she found herself yielding to the allure of frying bacon. A few slices would taste just right mixed with a bowl of Ethan's Cap'n Crunch cereal and a dollop of banana yogurt.

Ethan looked up from a video game. "Where's everyone going?"

"We're taking wreaths to the cemeteries, to Grandfather Peter's and your Pop Pop's graves. You'd better get off the computer and find your coat."

Paul and his parents spoke among themselves while slipping into their parkas and gloves.

Her son's lower lip quivered. "What about my dad's grave?"

Erin sucked in her breath, missing a poignant look between her new husband and his parents. "There's so much to do in preparation for Christmas and not enough time to go to Lansdale then get back in time for tonight's service."

"B-but, we can't forget Dad." A tear escaped, slipping down his cheek.

She held her arms out to her man-child, pulling him against her. "No, we can't, and we won't, not today, not ever. We have a wreath just for him, and we'll put it on his grave the day after Christmas. I'm so sorry I forgot to tell you. Forgive me?" Her heart pounded. What if her foul-up resulted in a spoiled Christmas for Ethan just when everything was starting to feel perfect again? Why did she plow ahead with her to-do list with such mental focus there wasn't room for common courtesy?

He pulled back and looked into her eyes. "Promise? You're not blowing smoke?"

Where had he picked up that expression? She had to smile. "I promise."

"Then I forgive you."

Supper was a hasty affair of cold cuts and deli salads after a luncheon feast at Settee Luna and last-minute food and gift preparations at home before they needed to pick up Audrey for church and her overnight stay. Erin fled upstairs to dress for the Christmas Eve service with only minutes to spare and no help from two derelict pairs of pantyhose with runs at the top. What was it lately with her and rogue pantyhose anyway? She tossed the flawed pairs into her trash can and dug deeply in her drawer.

When at last she presented herself to Paul, he didn't seem to mind she'd set the family back by eight minutes. His eyes glimmered at the sight of her, and he reached out for her hand and kissed it as if they were living in the eighteenth century instead of an era when people let doors slam in other people's faces. "You are so beautiful."

She dipped her chin. "Thank you, and you look very handsome." *A youthful B.J. Hunnicutt.* She glanced at Ethan, yanking at his necktie. "As for you, young man ..." She stopped herself from saying "You are perfect." Instead she chose, "You will make all the junior high girls swoon."

"He looks so much like you," Louise said with her quiet smile.

"Thank you." While Erin agreed, she didn't bother to add what she was thinking—*He's the spitting image of his father.* There had been enough awkwardness for one day.

Finding the pew they usually sat in occupied by a family Erin didn't recognize, Paul directed them to one a few rows behind. Louise slipped in first, followed by Tim, then Paul, Erin, Audrey, and Ethan. The organist was playing pre-service music Erin didn't recognize, but the melodic flourishes carried hints of the eighteenth century. In the sanctuary, aglow with candelabra against the backdrop of vibrant poinsettias and red altar cloths, her spirit merged with the quiet buzz of excited congregants, smiling to herself, inhaling the bouquet of pine boughs and perfume. *Whoever says Christmas is for children is wrong.* The oldest of people could experience the thrill of hope a baby wrapped in swaddling clothes and lying in a manger brought to a weary world.

A girl two rows ahead sneezed, and the elderly woman next to her fished in her purse for a tissue. Paul, having opened his bulletin, tapped Erin's shoulder and pointed to the entry under "Memorial Poinsettias" where she read, "In loving memory of Tony Pellerite and Jim Miles." She closed her eyes, nodding her head.

Noticing how radiant her mother appeared she said, "You look happy, Mom."

"Oh, Erin, when I sit here in this church, I am happy. I can almost feel my father's presence. Mother went to the Lutherans, but Father brought us kids here."

She could relate, though a bit differently. In this place, she experienced a continuity of the generations of her family who had come to this place through all the encircling years. She could picture her mom as a child with her siblings sitting up straight next to Erin's grandfather, who would make sure they all behaved during the service. And before that, he would have been the child attending worship with his parents, and all the way back to Grandfather Peter. *Maybe he sat in this very pew when Pastor Rodenheimer gave the congregation what-for on Christmas Eve 1781.* She shivered, but not from cold.

The organist paused after the last piece, then upped the volume and the pace with the opening strains of Erin's favorite Christmas carol, "Hark! the Herald Angels Sing." The congregation rose, hammering down on the first words of the centuries-old song as Pastor Stan and one of the elders processed down the center aisle. When they got to the third verse, just as she was singing, "born to raise the sons of earth, born to give them second birth," she froze when she spotted him on the opposite side of the church. Alone. Hunched. Looking down, lips barely moving over the open hymnbook. Craig Reldan. He appeared to be a hundred years old. Erin journeyed from the heights to a stomach tightening bottom of the well, but something inside barred the door to her earlier bitterness. She turned away from the sight of a broken man and said a prayer for him as Pastor Stan welcomed the congregation. The service continued with lessons and carols, although Erin frowned over some of the Scripture passages, which seemed to have nothing whatsoever to do with Christmas.

At last, the minister took his place in the church's raised pulpit to give his Christmas Eve message.

"You may wonder why I chose the passages I did for tonight. Second Samuel twelve and John twenty-one aren't exactly Christmas fare, are they?" he asked.

I think he must have read my mind.

"What do the stories of Peter's denial of Jesus and Nathan rebuking King David have to do with the birth of Jesus Christ?" Stan leaned over the pulpit. "I'll tell you. Everything."

He had Erin's attention.

"We all have seen the commercial of a woman cringing on the floor after a fall as she presses a button on a device around her neck and says, 'Help! I've fallen, and I can't get up.' She's us—she's me. She's you. We've all fallen from God's grace, from his rich fellowship, from his storehouse of blessings after following the devices and desires of our own hearts, and on our own we can't get up. Like Peter and David, none of us think such a thing will ever happen to us. Peter had just sworn to Jesus that even if all the other disciples fell away, he wouldn't. Only hours later under the scrutiny of a servant girl in a dimly-lit courtyard, Peter literally swore he never knew Jesus.

"We all, like Peter, like wandering sheep, have gone astray. We all are sinners. The great truth of Christmas is not about a perfect celebration or gifts, but that rather than washing his hands of us all and saying 'to hell with all of you,' Jesus volunteered to head up the greatest rescue mission in history."

Erin jumped at the pastor's almost expletive.

"He left the perfection of Heaven to enter the grit and drama of our cluttered, confused, chaotic lives. He came to redeem our estrangements, our divorces, our grief, our diseases of mind and body, our accidents, our joblessness, our contested elections, and our resentments.

"Most people today say there are many paths to God, that all religions lead to the same conclusion, that everyone goes to heaven. But only one path leads to a manger. And a cross. There is only one possible way, impossible as it may seem. This is the way we experience redemption. When we've fallen and we can't get up, there is only one nail-scarred hand to lift us and put us back on our feet."

Only then could Erin begin to breathe normally.

At the opening of the last hymn, "Silent Night," the church went dark. Pastor Stan lit a taper from the Christ candle at the center of the Advent Wreath, then each of the four ushers in turn dipped their candles to receive the flame. They carried their lights to the people in the pews, one after the other, the tiny sparkles filling the sanctuary with warmth and hope.

She stood there holding her candle, realizing what she needed to do. She wouldn't even run her idea by Paul, knowing in her heart he would understand. As soon as the carol ended and Pastor Stan released them with a benediction, she slipped out of her pew and made her way to the shattered man who couldn't seem to look up. "Merry Christmas, Craig."

He opened his eyes, gaped. "M-merry Christmas to you as well."

"Beautiful service, wasn't it?" She intuited his struggle. "If you don't have other plans, I'd love to have you join my family for Christmas dinner." She felt Paul's presence.

"Do come, Craig," he said.

"Well, I ... Are you sure?" The eyes flickered.

"Absolutely."

"Thank you. I would like that very much."

She could almost hear her grandfather Peter whisper, "Well done."

ABOUT THE AUTHOR

At fifteen, Rebecca Price Janney faced-off with the editor of her local newspaper. She wanted to write for the paper; he nearly laughed her out of the office. Then she displayed her ace—a portfolio of celebrity interviews she'd written for a bigger publication. By the next month she was covering the Philadelphia Phillies. During Rebecca's senior year in high school, *Seventeen* published her first magazine article and in conjunction with the Columbia Scholastic Press Association, named her a runner-up in their teen-of-the-year contest. She's now the award-winning author of twenty-five published books, including the Golden Scroll Award's Historical Novel of the Year for *Easton*

at the Crossroads, Easton at the Pass, as well as runners-up, *Morning Glory* and *Sweet, Sweet Spirit.* Her other books include *Easton in the Valley, Easton at the Forks, Sweet, Sweet Spirit: One Woman's Journey to the Asbury College Revival, Great Women in American History, Great Events in American History, Harriet Tubman, Then Comes Marriage?,* and *Who Goes There?*

A popular speaker, Rebecca regularly appears on radio shows and has a weekly podcast, "Inspiration from American History" at Anchor.fm/rebeccapricejanney. She's a graduate of Lafayette College, Princeton Theological Seminary, and Missio Seminary, where she received her doctorate, having focused on the role of women in American history. She lives with her husband, son, and Cavalier King Charles spaniel in Pennsylvania's Lehigh Valley.

GERMAN TRANSLATION

Chapter Three	
Heute haben wir Andrew begraben.	Today we buried Andrew.
Geboren, Gestorben	Born, died
Chapter Six	
Vorahnung	Premonition
Chapter Twelve	
Guten tag, Herr Kichline, Herr Rodenheimer!	Good day, Mr. Kichline, Mr. Rodenheimer!
Meine Tochter	My daughter
Sie ist meine Familie, mein Fleisch und mein Blut.	She is my family, my flesh and my blood.
Chapter Fourteen	
Ja, meine Tochter. Guten Tag, Herr Kichline, Frau Kichline!	Yes, my daughter. Good day, Mr. Kichline, Mrs. Kichline!
Meine Vater	My father

Kindern	Children
Danke. Vielen dank.	Thank you. Thank you very much.
Chapter Sixteen	
Entschuldigung?	Excuse me?
Chapter Eighteen	
Hausfrau	Housewife
Chapter Twenty	
Christ Kind	Christ Child
Geboren Ist Uns Der Heilige Christ	The Holy Christ was Born to Us
Liebling	Darling
Chapter Twenty-One	
Geschenk	Gift

OTHER BOOKS BY REBECCA PRICE JANNEY

EASTON SERIES (Elk Lake Publishing)

Easton at the Forks
Easton in the Valley
Easton at the Crossroads
Easton at the Pass

MORNING IN AMERICA SERIES (Elk Lake Publishing)

Morning Glory
Sweet, Sweet Spirit

Great Events in American History (AMG)
Great Women in American History (Moody)
Great Stories in American History (Horizon)
Great Letters in American History (Heart of Dakota)

Harriet Tubman (Bethany House)
Who Goes There? (Moody)
Then Comes Marriage? (Moody)

  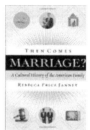

The Heather Reed Mystery Series (Word)
The Impossible Dreamers Series (Multnomah)

Rebecca would love to connect with you. To sign up for her monthly newsletter containing updates, contests, inspiration, and encouragement, send her an email through her website: www.rebeccapricejanney.com. Did you like the book? Please tell your friends and consider posting a review on Amazon.com.